MAR 13 1972

W9-BWH-352

How Long Is Always?

How Long Is Always?

BY LENORA MATTINGLY WEBER

Thomas Y. Crowell Company New York

Designed by Mahala Burck

Manufactured in the United States of America

L. C. Card: 75-101937

First Printing

BOOKS BY LENORA MATTINGLY WEBER

Meet the Malones
Beany Malone
Leave It to Beany!
Beany and the Beckoning Road
Beany Has a Secret Life
Make a Wish for Me: A Beany Malone Story
Happy Birthday, Dear Beany
The More the Merrier: A Beany Malone Story
A Bright Star Falls: A Beany Malone Story
Welcome, Stranger: A Beany Malone Story
Pick a New Dream: A Beany Malone Story
Tarry Awhile: A Beany Malone Story
Something Borrowed, Something Blue: A Beany Malone Story
Come Back, Wherever You Are: A Beany Malone Story
Don't Call Me Katie Rose
The Winds of March: A Katie Rose Story
A New and Different Summer: A Katie Rose Story
I Met a Boy I Used to Know: A Katie Rose Story
Angel in Heavy Shoes: A Katie Rose Story
How Long Is Always?

To Dave and Mary Weber in Chiddingford

How Long Is Always?

I

Stacy Belford knew exactly when her feeling of being out of tune with life started. It was a most unusual feeling for a girl whose family said she had been born under a dancing star and whose friends always marveled at how much bounce to the ounce she had.

It was on the day after the festive, happy last week of school, which was also the first week in June. She had been one of the junior escorts for the graduation class at St. Jude's High, and had worn a new turquoise dress, silver sandals, and a silver ribbon to hold back her long, auburn-blond hair. She had danced a strap loose on one of the sandals at the Auf Wiedersehen prom, and she had also met a boy with a thatch of thick dark hair, an off-center grin, and something both carefree and untouched in his brown eyes. He was with a Sing Out group, he told her, and if her house had porch steps, he'd sit on them and play his guitar for her.

But on this warm afternoon, the day after school's closing, she went back to St. Jude's to empty her gym locker. Her friend Claire, who had gathered up her belongings in the library, walked home with her.

Usually it was Stacy who told about the exciting events in her life and Claire who listened. But today Claire talked all the way from St. Jude's to Hubbell Street about her summer job in a small-town library fifty miles away. Strange, that certain superiority the goer-away feels for the stayer-at-home.

They halted on the corner outside the two-story Belford house. Stacy freed a hand from her load of gym shoes, shorts, and bulky sweat shirt to open the gate of the picket fence. "Come on in, Claire. You know how Mom always brews up tea at four."

"No, I have to hurry home and pack. I'll send you a card."

Having a good time. Wish you were here.

Before Stacy could close the gate, three young bicyclists, followed by a brown and white mongrel dog, came swerving around the corner, jumped their bicycles expertly onto the curb, and swished just as expertly through the gate. These were the Belford twins, Matt and Jill, and the slightly younger Brian. It took a second glance to tell which was which, what with their identical size, blue eyes, Levis, T-shirts, and ragged tennies. The family always lumped them together as "the littles."

Each had a bundle under his arm, and Jill, the spokesman for the three, imparted, "Grandda's coming in tomorrow to take us home with him. And Gran said we couldn't come unless we each of us brought tops and bottoms of pajamas to sleep in."

Brian, the youngest, gave Stacy his gentle smile. "You know how old people get funny ideas."

So the littles too were leaving town to visit their Irish grandparents in the small farming town of Bannon fifty-seven miles away. "How long are you going to stay?" Stacy asked.

The back door banged open, and the Belfords' mother came hurrying to the clothesline and unsnipped clothespins from a long and ruffled petticoat. "Honestly, if I'd ever remember. I meant to bring it in when it was just damp enough to iron. Now it's dry and stiff as a board, and I'll have to dampen it."

Their Irish relatives always said that Stacy was the "spittin' image" of her mother. They both had red hair, blue eyes decidedly on the greenish side, and the glowing translucent skin that often goes with red hair and that never takes a tan but burns to a painful crimson. They both had a spilling-over laugh, and both walked as though they were keeping time to music.

Since Stacy's father died over five years ago, Mother had been playing the piano at Guido's Gay Nineties nightclub on the outskirts of town. The petticoat she was lamenting over was the one she wore to hold out her old-fashioned billowing skirts, which along with her pompadour and lace mitts was part of the decor.

Jill asked, "Mom, how long did Grandda say we'd be staying out there?"

"He didn't say. But *I'd* say two weeks. That's about as long as anyone can put up with the three of you."

Mother unpinned slipovers and piled them on top of the load in Stacy's arms. "Give these to Katie Rose when you go upstairs. She's packing."

They walked in the back door together. Ben, the oldest of the six Belford children, was in the kitchen, rubbing Neetsfoot oil into the heavy work boots he had worn on a road-building crew last summer. He was starting on the same job tomorrow. He too had that certain superiority that being a wage earner gives a young person.

Since Mother had been widowed, Ben was her prop and mainstay. She was impulsive, loving, generous, and so quick-tempered the family had learned to dodge the pancake turner, hairbrush, or whatever she had in her hand. But she was also a pushover for any of their pleas. It was the tall, grim-eyed Ben who kept a tight rein on them. It was Ben who grounded the littles after a fighting scrape; who said to Stacy and her older sister, Katie Rose, "No, siree, you can't go out alone with a fellow on the first date."

It was Ben who now said to the littles, "Go up to your room and try on your pajamas. Be sure they're big enough before you take them to Bannon."

Stacy followed them up the stairs. In the room she shared with her sister, Katie Rose was down on her knees wiping out a scuffed suitcase with a damp cloth. Her small blond poodle watched every move with a proprietary air. Katie Rose turned her attention to the armload Stacy dumped onto the bed. "They say the evenings are cool up there at camp. Can I take your sweat shirt?"

"Listen to who's talking. After all your la-de-da airs about anyone wearing *your* clothes."

Katie Rose's deep blue eyes stared in surprise at this ungenerous outburst from someone who heretofore had never cared who wore her clothes.

Stacy flung out, "I wish I was going away. Everybody else is while I stay home and swivel on the vine."

No one could mispronounce, misuse, or garble words the way Stacy could. Her family and the nuns at St. Jude's were forever correcting her. Katie Rose said automatically, "You'll either *shrivel* on the vine or *wither* on the vine, but you won't *swivel.*"

"Yes, I will. I'm swiveling already."

Mother called up the stairs for one of them to come down and make the tea while she ironed her petticoat. Katie Rose said—again with the superiority of an older sister, who had graduated from high school in cap and gown two days ago and who had a job at a girls' summer camp—"You, Stacy. I have to pack, because I'm being picked up in the morning. And guess what? The head counselor said I could bring Sidewinder."

The small poodle twisted himself joyfully. Katie Rose insisted that he understood everything she said.

So even the poodle was going someplace.

Stacy made the tea in the big earthenware pot, using a saucedish to take the place of the lid that was long since broken. She poured it for all the family as they gathered at the dinette table.

Mother set her cup on the ironing board. "I'm on the homestretch now," she said.

Again Stacy grumbled, "I wish I had a job for the summer."

"You've got your baby-sitting jobs," Ben said.

"Baby-sitting, phuff! I'm too old for baby-sitting. And I'm so sick-sick-sick of changing diapers I could gag."

"Too bad about you," Mother flared. "So am I sick-sick-sick of thumping out 'Auld Lang Syne' over and over at the club. Everybody in town is having hail-and-farewell parties. I've played all those tearjerkers till I could gag."

Mother was always snappish when she ironed what she called her three-mile petticoat. She added more sympathetically, "But you have your morning driving job, Stacy. You like that."

Stacy not only baby-sat for the Novaks across the street, but she also drove the man of the house the thirteen miles to the Federal Center each morning and then brought the car back so that his wife could use it for errands. Mr. Novak returned in the evening with one of his co-workers.

Stacy reached for the outside crust of the bread and shook her head with added gloom. "Not after tomorrow I won't. Didn't I tell you? Now that school is out, Mrs. Novak will load the kids in the car and drive him out herself."

After a cup of tea and a thick slice of Mother's Irish bread, Ben departed to have the family Chevy checked over. He would be driving it to his job early in the morning. The littles gathered up crumbs for the white mice in their room upstairs and scrambled off the long dinette bench. Mother poured herself fresh tea and sat down.

Katie Rose was now at the ironing board, pressing skirts and blouses. "I have news for you, Stacy. Your onetime lover boy, Bruce, won't be home this summer."

"Where'd you hear that?"

"Straight from the horse's mouth—Bruce's father. Mr. Seerie told Jeanie, and Jeanie told me." (Jeanie was Katie Rose's intimate friend.) "He said that he and Bruce's mother decided it would be well for Bruce to stay on with the Seerie relatives in Lincoln all summer because he's in with a group of water skiers and such. And then he's to enroll at Nebraska U this fall. You ought to know how his parents arrange all life's details for him."

"Yes—I know."

Mother snorted out, "Well, the Seeries needn't think Stacy's losing any sleep over whether their son stays or comes." But she gave her an anxious, motherly look.

"They know that Stacy called it quits with

Bruce last fall," Katie Rose put in. "Don't tell me they didn't pack him off to Lincoln right away for fear he wouldn't take it for quits."

What Katie Rose said of Bruce's mother and father was true. They did plan his life for him, and a redheaded girl named Stacy Belford didn't fit in with their plans. It was true too that it was Stacy who had called it quits. But she and Bruce had come to the point where they bickered and nagged and fought, where each parting ended in anger, and each meeting with apologies. "We do awful things to each other, Bruce," she had told him tearfully the evening they said good-bye.

It was true too that Stacy wasn't losing any sleep over the separation. Life was too full. But she felt an empty lack at hearing that Bruce wasn't coming back. She hadn't called it quits for always and always. There was still the vague hope that they could come together again and feel the old rhapsody without that queer nagging rancor between them.

What would a summer be like without Bruce and his cream-colored convertible and their going to Coral Sands? Without Stacy swimming and trying to keep her skin from blistering while Bruce water-skied or scuba-dived?

On a new rush of discontent, she got up to reach for the morning *Call* on top of the refrigerator. She turned to the Help Wanted section and ran a seeking finger down the first column. And the second.

Goodness, how untrained, how inexperienced a high-school junior was. *Keypunch oprs, ass't bookkeeper, beautician with following, legal sec, lab tech—* "Katie Rose, Mom, what does 'oppty adv' mean?"

Mother answered, "Opportunity for advancement."

Stacy passed right over the liberal sprinkling of ads for barmaids—sometimes it was dressed up to read, "Cocktail waitress." Even if her age weren't against her, Ben would put his size-twelve foot right down on those.

Suddenly she sat up straighter and read one of the ads through a second time:

Unusual job for unusual girl, 18 or up. Must be good driver, have strong character and tact. Send details of self and family, recent picture or snap. Interview only by app't.

It gave the name Judge Kenneth McKibben and a downtown address.

Stacy drew a catchy breath. "I'm going to answer this unusual job for unusual girl. Listen." She read the ad aloud. "I'm a good driver. Mr. Novak says I'm better than his wife or the man he rides home with. What does tact mean?"

Mother answered, "It means saying the right thing at the right time. And knowing when to open your mouth and when to keep it shut. Judge McKibben. He was in your father's class at the university. It won't hurt to answer it, Stacy, but don't build any hopes on getting it. There'll be hundreds of answers." She took her petticoat in to the sewing machine in the living room to mend a rent in it.

Stacy, with Katie Rose's help, wrote her application:

I am a student at St. Jude's High School, and am going on eighteen.

Well, if you were sixteen going on seventeen, you were also going on eighteen, weren't you?

For six months I have driven our neighbor, Mr. Novak, to the Federal Center thirteen miles out of Denver.

To show her strong character, she added,

Even when Mr. Novak is short of time, I never exspeed the speed limit.

Katie Rose changed her *exspeed* to *exceed.* "Seems like it ought to be exspeed," Stacy said.

A late picture or snapshot. The one for the yearbook was too large to go into an ordinary envelope. She looked through snapshots. Why did she have to look so *grinny* in all of them? No, none of these cheer-leader ones with her twirling a megaphone or leaping high in the air. And none of these in her basketball togs, looking so idiot young and hoydenish. Ah, here was the one Jill had snapped with her new camera Easter morning. Dressed for church, Stacy looked not only suitably garbed but suitably grave.

As she went out the front door to mail the letter on the Boulevard five blocks away, their next-door neighbor came out of his gate. Mr. Stegman was a dapper little man, a retiree who worked part-time in a small hotel on Broadway. Today was his day off.

"Are you going downtown, Mr. Stegman?"

"Yes, Stacy. There's some pressing business I have to transact."

(Mother had said once, "Bless his heart. The pressing business he has to transact is probably paying the phone bill.")

"Would you mind mailing a letter for me? It'll be picked up a lot quicker than if I mailed it on the Boul."

"I'll be happy to, little lady."

Stacy thanked him and turned back to the house as though she too had pressing business. Mr. Stegman considered himself quite a wit and drew from a stock of moth-eaten jokes. Mother had told the young Belfords, "I know, I know they're at least fifty years old, but laugh anyway. Let me catch any of you acting as though the poor fellow's a bore, and I'll bash your head in."

Mr. Stegman returned later. Mother swirled herself around on the piano bench in front of their hard-used upright to call, "Come in." A banquet honoring a retiring school principal was being held at the Gay Nineties club this evening, and she was practicing the song the music teacher at the school had composed for the occasion.

Stacy with Jill's grumbling help was getting supper. Katie Rose was exempt because as a goer-away she had more important things to do. Stacy pushed into the hall to hear Mr. Stegman report that he had dropped her letter into a rapid delivery box downtown. "So it's being delivered just about now."

Even after Stacy had thanked him, the wit of Hubbell Street lingered on to ask, "Did I ever tell you about the fellow I knew who came in from the country to buy a record? So he went into the music store and said he wanted a record with 'Has Anybody Here Seen Kelly?' on the front side and 'I Wonder Who's Kissing Her Now' on the back side."

Mother threw back her head and laughed. Stacy managed a half-hearted one. Mr. Stegman like a good actor exited on his curtain line.

"Whiskers a foot long," Stacy muttered.

Mother gave another gust of laughter. "I know. No one has seen Kelly, and no one wonders who's kissing her now—front side or back side—in fifty years. That's why it's so funny."

Stacy baby-sat with the small Novaks across the street that night while their parents went to a party. As usual the children begged her to make fudge. Stacy's fudge was generally either hard and grainy or not hard enough. Tonight they ate it with spoons. The two oldest children argued over which TV show they should watch. The baby, almost too old for a bottle, pulled the nipple off it in protest at not being allowed to stay up.

The Novaks' homecoming was as usual too.

Mr. Novak had drunk a little too much, so that his wife treated him with lofty contempt. Stacy tried to duck out, but as usual Mr. Novak came stumbling after her, bellowing, "I wouldn't let a little girl like you go across the street alone at this time of night."

Stacy had become quite adept at opening their picket gate, sliding through it, and closing it before he realized it. But tonight their dog Cully got in her way. Mr. Novak grabbed her arm, and even though she twisted away from him, she caught his whisky breath full force as his kiss grazed her chin.

She answered his "You don't think I'm a slob, do you, darlin'?" with an automatic "No, Mr. Novak," and left him holding on to the pickets.

Yet because she knew him for a warmhearted and generous man and because she sensed that his ego was flattened by his wife's cold disdain on these party nights, a defensive loyalty kept her from mentioning her dodgings to Katie Rose or her mother—much less to Ben, the rigid protector.

She walked slowly up the stairs and into the bedroom to the left. She was greeted by an odd and alien odor. Katie Rose, in bed but not asleep and with her hair in curlers, popped up to say, "It's my scuffed ballets I sprayed to turn them red. It says 'Instant Drying' on the can, but it doesn't say they keep on smelling like an operating room. It's ninety-five miles to the camp. Look there on our vanity at the new sunglasses I bought. You can have my old ones."

There was shivery excitement in Katie Rose's voice, the excitement of being poised on the edge of the nest, of trying wings for the first time, of thinking, Tomorrow night, I'll be ninety-five miles away and sleeping in a different bed.

Stacy's discontent was almost pain. *I don't want your old sunglasses. I don't want to go on sleeping in this same bed in this same room and having to laugh at Stegman's old moth-eaten jokes and dodging Novak's same old whisky kisses. I want to go away, too. I want to be me, Stacy Belford.*

2

The next morning Stacy ate a bowl of oatmeal while she watched out the window facing the Novak bungalow. She saw Mr. Novak come out and walk toward the garage, and she got up and raced across the street.

In the bright morning light the man dressed in plaid jacket, dark slacks, and light shirt, and smelling of aftershave lotion, was a different man from the one who had craved her assurance last night that he wasn't a slob.

There was little conversation as Stacy drove west. He had taken a folder from his briefcase to study. She let him out in front of one of the great huddle of government buildings and drove back past the sentry at the gate.

A mysterious blue haze hung over the mountains. A meadowlark balanced itself on a roadside fence and burst into song. Stacy pursed her lips and whistled back. She wished she didn't have to return the car and herself to Hubbell Street. She wished she could just keep on going—and going.

She was almost home, and driving with slow reluctance, when she stopped at a Stop sign a few blocks from Hubbell. A man stood at the curb, waiting impatiently to cross the street. He was as old as Stacy's grandfather in Bannon and had the same weathered face. In his plaid shirt and cowhand boots he looked as though he didn't belong in the city. He also looked as though he weren't used to being afoot. Stacy leaned out of the car and called out, "Would you like a lift someplace?"

He touched his wide-brimmed hat, and his leathery face crinkled with his smile. "That's nice of you, girlie, but I'm just going after some pipe tobacco to kill time."

Girlie! How corny could an old Westerner get? The driver behind Stacy honked impatiently, and she drove on.

She parked the car in the Novak driveway, noticing as she did so the long, gray, and dusty station wagon in front of her own house. The three young Belfords came streaking across the street, shouting, "He came about a job for you. See that man there on the porch talking to Mom. He's a judge. So hurry up."

She hurried. A young man sat in the back seat of the station wagon. As she passed, he lifted his eyes from some papers or a book in his lap and gave Stacy a detached smile—the kind of smile she seldom received from a man under thirty. She returned it in kind. The schoolteacher type with glasses that gave him an owlish look would never make *her* heart pound faster. She preferred the football hero or the life-of-the-party type.

Katie Rose was waiting on the porch beside her suitcase. She came out to meet Stacy with the anxious Sidewinder hugged close to her heels. "It's Judge McKibben," she hurried to impart. "He said he did get a whole stack of applications, but he remembered Mom and Dad at the University, and he said the name Belford was a recommendation in itself. Now do watch about pronouncing words, Stacy."

Her mother introduced Stacy to the judge. He shook hands with her. She was suddenly frightened. His eyes seemed to be X-raying her for the strong character and tact she had claimed. He spoke clearly and swiftly as though he were pressed for time.

"Let me explain things briefly before my father returns. He's a cattleman out near Starbrush—that's out east on the plains. Two weeks ago he came up to town for some dental work. And his first day in town he got four—that's right, four—traffic citations. Exceeding the speed limit, making a U-turn on our busiest boulevard, driving on a one-way street, and parking downtown where it said 'No Parking.' "

"Ah, the poor fellow," Mother said. "It's easy for someone from out of town to make mistakes. But he didn't hurt anyone, did he?"

"No, but he practically broke all records in the number of points he piled up against himself as a driver." A wintry smile flicked across the judge's face. "And it didn't help matters for him to cuss out all the officers and court officials. So the board took his license away for ninety days. He wants to get back to the ranch today, and he has to have a driver for that and for all his running back and forth after he gets there. If he's caught behind the wheel again, it could mean a permanent loss of license. He had to come back to the dentist yesterday, and I realized I had to hire a new driver for him because he doesn't get along with the one who's been driving for him and—"

Mother broke in, "Wouldn't a man driver be better?"

The judge shook his head emphatically, and nodded toward the studious young man in the car. "I made arrangements with Fabian there to drive him. Fabian is a university student whose home is in Starbrush." Again that flick of rueful smile. "But let's face it. Father is a bully. He'd get impatient and tell Fabian that if he didn't get out of the driver's seat and let him drive, he'd throw him out. And he would."

"Doesn't your mother drive?" Mother broke in again. "I should think she'd be the logical one to drive for your father."

For the first time the judge seemed at a loss for words. He even took longer to clear his throat than seemed necessary. "I don't suppose you've heard about Starbrush celebrating its Centennial this year. Mother is a descendant of the Starbrush who founded the town, and she's taken on the job of restoring the Starbrush house and making it into a museum."

Mother's "Oh-h" seemed to question whether a wife couldn't still find time to drive her husband wherever he needed to go. The judge changed the subject with, "My wife got the idea of hiring a girl driver for Father."

Again his X-ray eyes turned on Stacy, and she confessed, "I upped my age a year when I answered your ad."

"But you drive well. I watched you as you came down the street and put the car away."

"She's so young," Mother demurred, "and she's never been away from home—and Starbrush is so far."

"A hundred and eighty-two miles. We don't think it's far. I drive out and back the same day. Here comes Dad now."

It was the plaid-shirted, booted man to whom Stacy had offered a ride who was coming down Hubbell Street.

"I'm not too young, Mom, if Judge McKibben doesn't think so. I'd like the job. I like his father. I offered him a ride, and he called me girlie. And, Judge, even if he did tell me to get out of the driver's seat and let him drive, I wouldn't. I mean, he'd have to throw me out, and I don't think he would."

"No, he wouldn't. He wouldn't lay a finger on you."

Mother showed signs of wavering. "I just wish Ben were here."

Stacy was thankful he was out building roads, and not here to slam shut her door on which "oppty" was knocking. "Please, Mom, I've just been praying for a job. Everybody else has, and I'd just—"

Katie Rose kicked her on the shin in time to keep her from saying "—swivel on the vine."

By now the weathered cattleman had turned in at the Belfords'. He came up the porch steps. He had evidently met the others in the family. The judge started to introduce Stacy, but he said with a roguish grin, "We've met already. She's the only person in this overgrown town that's offered me a ride."

His son asked, "What would you think of my hiring her to drive you back to Starbrush and chauffeur you around the country till you get your license back?"

The old man gave Stacy a quick appraising glance, and his smile crinkled his tanned face again. "That's fine—just fine with me. But I've got to get going as soon as we can. I have to see some Hereford breeders in Starbrush around five." He had an impatient way of talking, of pacing up and down as he did so. "How about it, girlie, how soon can you get ready?"

"I can be ready in a jiff. Just wait till I pack some clothes." She was through the door as she said it. She took the steps two at a time.

Mother's leather suitcase, full of Katie Rose's belongings, was sitting on the front porch. The large one with the zippered plaid-cloth side had already been preempted and partly filled by the littles for their visit to their grandparents. That left only a Mexican tote bag of woven hemp with gaudily bright stripes. Stacy didn't mind. She'd have been happy to throw her clothes into a gunnysack.

Jill came up to tell her that Mother said for her to wear a skirt for the drive to Starbrush. Stacy fastened a green wraparound over her white shorts.

Katie Rose, still uncalled for by the head counselor, came up to report progress below stairs. "The judge is talking to Mom while he's waiting for a taxi to take him to his office. He's going to pay you thirty dollars a week, and it'll be ten weeks before his father gets his license back, and it'll all be clear profit because you'll get your board, and Judge McKibben says his mother's a marvelous cook."

Stacy stood, a shoe in one hand and a wadded-up night-gown in the other, and stared in round-eyed amazement. She hadn't really thought about money before. She had thought only of getting out of the baby-sitting class and her protected nest.

She breathed out, "Is ten weeks times thirty dollars really three hundred?"

"Of course it is, idiot."

"Katie Rose, I'll *give* you my sweat shirt. I'll be rich. I'll buy everybody everything his or her heart desires. I'll be rich and a woman of the world when I come back."

"Stop wadding in your clothes like that. Don't

forget your junior escort dress, in case you go to something swank. Did you notice the boy in the car?"

"Boy? He's old and squint-eyed."

"He is not squint-eyed. He's working on his doctorate at Colorado U. He's going back to Starbrush and live in his grandmother's house not far from the McKibben ranch. He's been hired to make the Centennial celebration a big success. His doctorate is in lit, so for heaven's sake, don't go mispronouncing words."

"What do you want me to do? Keep my mouth shut all the hundred and eighty-two miles to Starbrush?"

"Just don't use words over two syllables."

Mother came into the bedroom with a new pair of stockings someone had given her and a five-dollar bill. She pressed them both on Stacy.

"No, Mom, you keep the five. I won't need it. I've got my baby-sitting money from the Novaks."

"Take it—you never know—" Mother's voice broke.

"Ah, for Pete's sake. What's there to cry about? I'll only be gone ten weeks."

"But you're leaving home. I remember when I left. I changed—things happen to change you—and home looks so different when you come back. Oh, my dear own, you're so young—and green—and I suppose I ought to give you some going-away advice—"

"Oh, no, Mom—not the love life of the rooster now."

One of the littles called up to say that the judge wanted to say good-bye to Mother and she left, blinking back tears, and muttering that she wouldn't have dared talk to her mother the way her children. . . .

Katie Rose went downstairs too, taking the sweat shirt from Stacy to crowd into her suitcase.

Stacy picked up the bulky Mexican bag. She glanced about the dismantled room that suddenly looked bereft and impersonal with the mirror, spray cologne, lipstick, and jewelry gone from the dressing table. How neat the bed looked with no dents from sitting on it, no curled-up Sidewinder. On the open closet door, the shoe bag showed gaps like missing teeth. She kicked the door shut before she left the room.

Mercury with wings on his heels had nothing on Stacy Belford as she tripped down the stairs with the woven striped bag thumping against her knees. *Here I come, world, on a dead run.*

3

Mother, the littles, Katie Rose (and, of course, Sidewinder) went with Stacy and Mr. McKibben to the car. The bookish young man whose name was Fabian Brown got out and took Stacy's unwieldy bag. He crowded it into the back with some old picture frames and small pieces of furniture.

"I've gathered up all these battered furnishings for the Starbrush museum that's to open on Centennial Day," he explained. "I've been hired to do the legwork for it."

Jill pointed to an unrecognizable object and asked, "My gosh, what's that?"

"A stereopticon to sit on top of that marble-topped table when I get it patched up." He handed it to her. "Look at the slide of Niagara Falls through it."

"Heavens and earth," Mother said. "Those were old when I was a girl."

"Trash," Mr. McKibben snorted. "Trash, people threw out fifty years ago."

Good-byes were said, and Stacy took her place

behind the wheel. She pulled the seat forward to fit her smaller height, and started off.

She had driven their own rattly Chevy and the Novaks' fairly new Ford. She had taken the wheels of the jalopies, the sport cars, and the minis of the boys she dated. But never before had she handled a car so long or powerful as the gray McKibben station wagon. Nor had she ever driven with a passenger behind her whom she had replaced, and with another beside her who was the car's owner and her boss and whose hands fairly twitched to take hold of the wheel himself.

The front seat didn't stay forward but slid back as she turned the first corner. She worked it forward again to the accompaniment of Mr. McKibben's "Pull it up—pull it up to suit you" only to have it stubbornly slip back. She finally gave up, even though it meant she must sit on the edge of the seat to reach gas and brake pedals.

On the highway, it was the slower-moving, unwieldy and hard-to-pass, even hard-to-see around campers and trailers that Stacy's boss was fidgety and irate about. It did seem as though all the world had taken to the road in them. "Look at that! Will you look at that! Coming out here from Arkansas and taking up the whole road."

Over a long stretch of up-and-down road, while the sun glared through Katie Rose's cast-off sunglasses, she had to stay behind a camper. It was a particularly wide and bulky homemade one, with children peering out the glass in the back door.

She might have got by it when it slowed maddeningly on the upgrades, but the yellow line in the middle of the road forbade passing.

"Go around him. Go ahead," ordered Mr. McKibben. "I can't stand poking along behind a damfool tourist."

"I can't. There's too much oncoming traffic," Stacy said.

For over an hour she sat taut on the edge of her seat, edging the car up while she peered around the white sides of the camper, only to fall behind again at the sight of an approaching car.

It was past noon when they reached the straggly little town of Pigeon Rock. "Stop here," Mr. McKibben told her. "This is the halfway mark. There—park there in the shade in front of the courthouse." He was already out of the car, but he called back over his shoulder, "Get yourself lunch in the café—they make good doughnuts here. Go on, both of you, I have to drop in and see Dan Sweeney."

Fabian Brown opened the car door for her and helped her out. Her wobbly legs would scarcely bear her weight. She put her hands behind her and flexed fingers that were cramped from clutching the wheel. He gave her arm a gentle shake. "Relax, young'un. You're doing fine."

The muscles in her arms twitched, her head ached. . . . Nor had she given thought to the strain and fatigue that went with *holding* a job. . . . She stumbled across the street to the café with Fabian.

"I thought maybe you'd be mad at me for taking your job."

He chuckled. "No, ma'am, I'm not mad about it. I never wanted the job in the first place. I'm glad about it."

She sat with him at a round metal table in the lunchroom. But she whose appetite seldom failed her was too tense and shaky to be hungry. Fabian ordered coffee and doughnuts from the boy who came for their order. Stacy only wanted tea. The boy asked Fabian if his ducks liked stale apple pie, and Fabian said he'd never found anything they didn't like.

He told Stacy about his ducks while they waited for their order. She sensed that he was talking to give her a chance to pull her shaky self together.

"I lived with my grandmother on her little place at Starbrush when I was a kid. I was about fourteen when I happened to read a poem by William Allingham—about ducks on a pond and a blue sky above. It ended,

> 'What a little thing
> To remember for years,
> To remember with tears,'

and I suddenly felt that life would be more beautiful with ducks on a pond. So I got a pair of baby ducks from Mrs. Lauderbach, and named the she-duck after her, and I worked all summer to widen old Rattlesnake Creek—it runs just below Grandma's house—and make a pond. And my Mrs. Lauderbach begot little ducks, and would you believe it? the old matriarch of the flock is still alive and talking back to me."

The boy brought their coffee, tea, and doughnuts, as well as a paper sack of offerings for the ducks. Fabian showed her about putting the tea bag in the miniature teapot of hot water.

"Our teapot would make twenty of those," she commented.

"I don't suppose you use tea bags at home."

"Goodness, no. Mom thinks they're socko-religious."

She heard his "Do you mean sacrilegious?" and blushed crimson.

"Katie Rose told me not to use words with more than two syllables. I'm color-blind and tone-deaf about words. I pronounce them the way I think they ought to be pronounced."

"You and Shakespeare. That's the way new words are born."

They had no sooner finished their scanty lunch than a bus stopped outside and its passengers surged in, crowding the small space.

"That's the bus that goes through Starbrush—the Kansas City to Denver one. It's late today. Let's wait in the car until Mr. McKibben shows up. It'll be cooler and quieter."

As he held the car door open for her, she saw him clearly for the first time. Fabian Brown. You could call him Medium Brown. He was of medium height, neither tall nor short. Of medium build, neither plump nor skinny. His hair was medium brown, and so were his eyes behind the glasses, and so was his sports jacket. His smile was medium, too —not as recklessly wide as the smiles of the younger boys Stacy knew.

He settled himself again in the back seat among the antique odds and ends as well as Stacy's large and garishly striped bag.

Stacy said, "Every so often you see about some town having a Centennil on TV, but I always turn it off. I don't like old things or old times."

His sensitive mouth quirked at the corners. "No, you're not the type. You're going to get quite a dose of Centennial at Starbrush, so let me explain it briefly."

My, he did sound schoolteacher-ish and may I have your attention, please!

"A hundred years ago on August twenty-third when a wagon train was headed for the gold diggings, Enos Starbrush's wagon broke down crossing a river. So he and his family had to stay behind. Other outfits as they came along laid over, too— there was good hunting and fishing—and the first thing you know a town got started named after Starbrush. Incidentally he was Mrs. McKibben's great-grandfather, and she's dedicated herself to refurnishing his old home and turning it into a museum to open on Centennial Day."

"Are you dedicated, too?"

Again that tucked-in smile. "Not exactly. I'm just doing a job I'm getting paid for."

"What's that book you've got that's about to fall apart?"

"This is called *Petals That Fall*—and the 'petals' are poems set to music, both composed by Milly, daughter of old Enos. Mrs. Mac is trying to bring her to life as the Songbird of Starbrush."

"Are the 'petals that fall' any good?"

He shook his head. "No, I haven't been moved by any. Overly sentimental. Most of them a sort of watered-down Thomas Moore. Do you know his poetry and songs?"

She sang out in her melodious soprano about the harp that once through Tara's Halls the soul of music shed. "Mom knows music from opera to rock 'n roll," she explained. "And I have an uncle who says that playing and singing come as natural to an O'Byrne—my mother was an O'Byrne—as howling to a dog. But I don't read," she confessed. "I hear Katie Rose say, 'I just couldn't put that book down.' Well, I just can't pick one up."

"But you had to read books at school and make reports on them?"

Again a guilty red suffused her face. "My friend Claire is also a reader, and sometimes I'd wade through the first and last chapter and she'd fill me in on what happened between. I did that with *Pride and Perjurious*, but I couldn't even slog through three pages of *Silas Mariner*."

He chuckled deeply. "You're wonderful. And because you are, I'll spare you my lecture on how reading opens doors to new worlds. Or maybe you don't need a new one when your own is so good."

Stacy, anxious to get off the subject of her lacks, asked, "Judge McKibben said your home was at Starbrush. Do you have a family there?"

"Do you mean am I married and do I have a family of my own?"

"You're old enough to have one, aren't you?"

"Yes, I'm old enough. Most of the boys and girls I went through High with in Starbrush already have kids frisking about. I'm going on twenty-seven. That's prehistoric to a sixteen-year-old, I'm sure."

"I'm going on seventeen," she corrected. "Are you going steady with a girl that you're going to marry?"

"No, I'm not going steady. And no, young'un, I'm not thinking of getting married."

"Why?"

"Because I wouldn't insult a girl by asking her to wait for me. I did once, and the girl gave me the merry ha-ha. I've still got a year—maybe two—before I get my doctorate. The reason I haven't got it at my present ripe old age is because I'd go to school a year and then teach a year to make money."

"Don't you have any family to help you?"

"My mother and father were killed in an auto accident in Mexico when I was in kindergarten. That left me on Grandma Brown's hands, and I wasn't exactly a welcome addition, and I don't wonder. Grandma has always had an itchy foot, and she had to stay put while Grandpa was alive and laid up with arthritis. So now she lives on her little place near the McKibbens' at Starbrush through the winter, and come spring she gets in her car and takes off. Yellowstone Park, Carlsbad Caverns, Aztec Ruins. So if I can pick up a summer job around Starbrush, I hole in there and look after the place and the ducks. There you have Fabian Brown's life story."

The passengers were now straggling out and climbing aboard the bus. Stacy was suddenly conscious that it was two hours past noon, that she still had the last half of the distance to Starbrush to drive, and that her boss wanted to be there before five. "Where do you suppose Mr. McKibben went?"

"He's three doors down from the café there in the Red Horse. He went there because he can't eat much with what he calls his cussed contraption—meaning a new partial plate. Sweeney probably fixed him up with an eggnog or something he didn't have to chew."

"Would you go and tell him we ought to be leaving?"

"That's your job, young'un. Besides, I wouldn't get to first base. Except to hear some of his choice vocabulary. He doesn't like me."

"Why?"

He hesitated a moment at her question. "You wouldn't understand if I told you now," he said.

Stacy found her boss in the dim light of the Red

Horse. He was relaxed in a booth, visiting with a bald-headed, jovial man. Mr. McKibben stood up when she stood beside him. "Dan, this is the nice little lady who's driving for me because the gestapo in Denver took away my license. Like a ginger ale, girlie?"

She shook her head on her thanks and reminded him that he wanted to be in Starbrush by five. "That's right," he agreed amiably and walked out with her.

At least, she thought as she drove out of Pigeon Rock, she wouldn't be harassed by that wide, homemade camper and the two children staring at her from its back door.

But there were other harassments.

They came upon a stretch of road-building and were waved to a stop with other eastbound cars. It was only a ten-minute wait, but it seemed longer with Mr. McKibben thrashing restively in the front seat. When they were finally motioned on, Stacy crept slowly over the thick coating of gravel and heard the rat-a-tat of pebbles against the bottom of the car.

The glare of the sun gave way to a dark and ominous sky. Thunder crackled close overhead, and the lightning flashes seemed alarmingly near. Then came a blinding downpour that the windshield wipers couldn't handle for a time. Again Stacy inched the car along, her heart in her throat. The rain came to a sudden stop, and the sun pushed out in full force.

Mr. McKibben dozed in the front seat, wakened, dozed again, pretending that he had never lost consciousness. Once when he emitted a catchy snore, Stacy caught Fabian's wink in the mirror.

Her edge-of-the-seat driving put such an ache in her back and between her shoulders that she wondered if she dared take time to stop and stretch. No, because the dashboard clock said five o'clock. Just then both Mr. McKibben and Fabian Brown spoke, "That's Starbrush there—right ahead."

4

Stacy didn't know what she expected from a cattle town, but Starbrush's Main Street was like a few blocks of College Boulevard where the Belfords shopped—a drugstore on one corner, a Laundromat on the other, the usual shoe store, liquor store, movie house, and beauty shop.

On College Boulevard, however, you wouldn't see a sign "Baby Chicks, Ducks Today. Week-old Turks Monday." You wouldn't worry for fear a bale of alfalfa would topple off the high load on the truck ahead of you. Mr. McKibben motioned her to turn right and cross the railroad tracks to the stockyards. "You come by for me in half an hour," he said as he climbed out. And in a city you wouldn't hear that bawling din of fenced-in cattle.

Fabian then directed her to the museum. The old Starbrush home was a shabby, yellow frame house, in need of fresh paint, and it sat in a square surrounded by cottonwood trees. "That brownish building next to the Starbrush house is the first school, and the other white one with the steeple is the first church. The buildings have all been moved to this block."

"I'll stay in the car. Remember? I don't like old relics."

His schoolteacher voice again. "It'll do you good to move around. I only want to see if Mrs. Mac is here and unload this marble top before something happens to it."

Stacy thought even less of old relics after one look around at the awful shambles and clutter of the Starbrush museum in the making. In the parlor-to-be an old organ was shrouded in a torn and faded green chenille bedspread. A platform rocker had one arm broken off, and its stuffing was leaking out of the back.

Mrs. McKibben had left about an hour ago, the women workers told Fabian.

There was a further jumbled melee in the bedroom-to-be. The woman who had evidently taken over the furnishing of it showed Fabian and Stacy a pillow sham, yellowed with age, with faded embroidery that read, "I Slept and Dreamed That Life Was Beauty."

"If only I could find the twin to it," the woman lamented.

Stacy, trying to show interest, murmured, "I didn't know pillow shams had twins."

Oh, yes. The woman as a child remembered her grandmother having a pair of them on her bed. The twin to this one had been embroidered to read, "I Woke and Found That Life Was Duty."

Once inside, there was no getting away. The women workers wanted to know what Fabian had accomplished on his two-day trip to Denver. They had to show him their finds.

Stacy's back ached and her ears hummed. She was so hollow. She wished she had bought a candy bar or two at Pigeon Rock. She wished she could drive on to the McKibben ranch where she could relax.

Another woman—Stacy judged that the kitchen was her major project—insisted on showing her and Fabian the old cookstove she and her husband had unearthed. "We found it tucked back in a dugout over in the Hay Gulch country," she told them happily.

The stove had evidently in its long and scarred life lost a back leg. The husband was hunkered down, fitting a block of wood under it to take the place of the missing leg. He looked up to say sourly to Fabian, "No reason why this won't do. Frozen-face seems to think I can whip up a curved leg out of a tire iron—or maybe a can opener."

"Now, Charlie, now—" his wife placated him.

"Let's go, Fabian," Stacy pleaded.

The Starbrush house had both a back and a front door. As Fabian slid the bolt off the back one, Stacy asked, "Who does that man mean when he says Frozen-face?"

He paused before answering, holding the door open. Suddenly he pulled her back, closed the door, and instead of answering her question, asked her,

"Do you feel up to being given a grand rush by a couple of girl-hungry boys you wouldn't be able to shake yourself loose from under an hour?"

"You mean they're outside?"

"Um-hmm, passing by."

"No, not now. I'm so achy—and so hungry. All I want is to get the car home and wash the dust off my face."

He reached over and kneaded her back with strong fingers. He did the same with her neck and shoulders. "You do look bushed. That help any?"

She nodded gratefully, and he said, "We can go now. The Lochinvars have driven on."

She drove back to the stockyards, worrying for fear she had kept her new boss waiting for her. He wasn't waiting, but she and Fabian had to spend another weary half hour, before he disengaged himself from a knot of men in the cattle corral and got in the car. "It's only eleven miles from home, girlie."

Fabian directed her, "Get back on the main drag again, and then turn right at the filling station." She drove seven miles due east after the turn. Fabian tapped her shoulder. "See that old caved-in sod church ahead? Turn north there."

Before long Mr. McKibben was gesturing to the left. "My land. My fences are all four-strand barbed wire. Keep going till you see a lot of white cattle sheds and pens. And you'll see and smell my white-faced Herefords. You ever see a prize-winning bull?"

"No."

"Wait'll you see Prince Eric."

The sun was dropping low when Stacy turned off the road and stopped while Fabian opened the barbed-wire gate. She drove on to the ranch holdings. There were the gleaming white cattle pens and a house with a V-shaped roof. It was also white but not so newly painted and gleaming. She stopped as Mr. McKibben directed under a giant cottonwood in front of the house.

The first to greet them was an old collie, shapeless as a bundle of fur, that waddled out in welcome. Stacy dropped her hands off the wheel and looked at the house set in its patch of green lawn. The door opened, and two people came out and crossed the porch that lay level with the ground. One was a tall, dark-haired girl about Stacy's age, wearing a purple slipover and slacks of bright psychedelic print. The other was a woman with hair more gray than brown, and she was wearing a pretty but durable pink dress.

Stacy had a nice feeling of having reached her destination, of coming home. In her mind she was already saying to the girl, "Golly, I didn't know whether my legs and back would last till I got here. I couldn't adjust the seat and—"

The slim dark-haired girl came dancing up to the car. "Surprise, Fabe. Surprise, Uncle Mac," she called out. "I guess you didn't expect to see me."

Fabian Brown extricated himself from the back seat and the antiques. "Hello, Eve. I'm used to being surprised by your bobbing up."

Mr. McKibben, flinging himself out of the front seat, asked only as he looked over her head at his cattle sheds where a workman with light, bushy hair was now standing, "When did you get here?"

"Yesterday. Aunt Evvy phoned and said for me to come. My boy friend drove me to the bus station in Denver—" She rolled her brown eyes and shrugged dramatically, "And so here is Little Eva."

Stacy turned to the woman who looked plump and pretty and motherly in her pink dress—white polka dots showed on a closer inspection. Fabian was filling his arms with assorted relics from the back seat. As he backed out of the car, the odd-shaped thing he had called a stereopticon slid off his load. Stacy caught it and held it.

Fabian said, "Mrs. Mac and Eve, this is Stacy Belford. She's taking my place as chauffeur for Mr. Mac."

Eve said, "Well, whatta you know!"

Stacy turned to Mrs. McKibben with a smile, disengaging her right hand from purse and stereopticon to shake hands.

The woman didn't return her smile, and she ignored the proffered hand. She also ignored Stacy's presence and spoke to Fabian, "*She's* going to chauffeur Mr. McKibben around! That's the most absurd thing I ever heard of. I sent for Eve to come out and drive him wherever he needs to go. We certainly don't need anyone else."

Stacy could only stand speechless. Fabian said, "Judge McKibben hired Stacy this morning."

"I don't know what he was thinking of. I phoned him yesterday afternoon to tell him Eve was here. I left a detailed message with his office girl that Eve—"

Eve interrupted with a gesture of upturned palms and her exaggerated shrug, "You know how it is, Aunt Evvy. I'm just not popular with the McKibben males."

And still Stacy was too overcome by her lack of welcome to say a word. She only stood, clutching her pouch bag and the stereopticon. Fabian momentarily diverted the woman's attention with, "I brought back a marble-topped table for your Enos Starbrush parlor. The table will need a lot of fixing, but the marble hasn't a crack—"

Eve demanded, "Isn't anyone else hungry? I'm absolutely famished. Isn't it about time we ate?"

"We've been waiting supper an hour," Mrs. McKibben said. "Come on in." But she didn't look at Stacy as she said it. "Eve, ring the supper bell for the men."

A bell fastened on a wooden arm outside the porch clanged as Eve jerked and rejerked the rope to it.

What could Stacy do or say? *But I'm Stacy Belford, and people always like me.* She could only walk on leaden feet beside Fabian to the door, which Mrs. McKibben was holding open. If only the woman would say, "You must be tired after your long drive."

She had all the earmarks of a capable, comfortable country woman, except for the grim set to her lips and the frosty blue of her eyes. And suddenly Stacy knew without asking Fabian. This was the woman the irate husband in the messy museum kitchen had referred to as Frozen-face.

5

The large room they stepped into was both dining and sitting room. It wasn't L-shaped, as those combination rooms often are in newer houses, but a plain rectangle with stairs to the second floor in one of its corners.

The supper table was already set. For *five,* Stacy noticed. There were already three on the McKibben ranch—the missus, her niece Eve, and the workman with the thick blond hair. So five places meant that they had expected only Mr. McKibben and Fabian Brown and *not* a driver by the name of Stacy Belford.

But Mother would make anyone welcome whether she was expected or not. Stacy felt her first twinge of homesickness.

Fabian and Mrs. McKibben had gone back to the car for the picture frames. Eve came racing in from the kitchen with an extra plate and silver.

Stacy said tentatively, "I like that outfit you've got on."

"Gaudy, but not cheap. I bought it with some

graduation money." (Graduation? Then Eve was a year or so older than she, Stacy realized.) "Is that an auburn rinse on your hair?" And after Stacy's shake of head, "Lucky you. Last summer I bleached mine, but a boy friend said it robbed me of my gypsy personality. I'm crazy about that new Capri Copper. I was just getting ready to use it—that is, I'd just about pried the money out of Dad—when Aunt Evvy phoned and said to come out here because Uncle Mac needed a driver."

"I'm sorry about that," Stacy said uncomfortably. "I'd like to wash up."

"The downstairs bath is through the kitchen. The upstairs one barely got underway when it was nipped in the bud." There was the sound of the men coming into the kitchen, and Eve added, "Here're the hungry farmers, so you'd better use the one upstairs. The guest room up there was also nipped in the bud, but that's where I sleep and where you'll be sleeping tonight."

The stairs led to a partly finished upstairs with the sloping ceiling of a half story. What Eve had called a guest room nipped in the bud was certainly just that. It had a doorway but no door. The walls were partly covered with thin building board. The floor had never been varnished or painted. There was no closet, only a few hooks to hang clothes on.

The room held one old iron bed, evidently occupied by Eve, for it was lumpily made with a tumble of clothes on top of it, and a cot under the window. The cot had only a cover on the mattress, a pillow without a pillow slip, and blankets folded at the foot. Even so, it looked inviting to Stacy's aching body.

The unfinished bathroom was as large as the bedroom, so that the toilet and small washbowl looked solitary and skimpy. There was no tub. Stacy turned on the hot water faucet over the bowl, and nothing happened. She turned on the cold, and a small stream of water gurgled out.

The sloshing of cold water on her face refreshed her. Maybe by now Mrs. McKibben had got over the shock of seeing a new girl driver. Maybe it would clear the air if she asked Mr. McKibben right out if he wanted her, Stacy, or his niece Eve to drive the station wagon for him.

But her courage failed her at sight of Mrs. McKibben. It was Eve who said it for her as they took their places at the table. "Fine thing, Uncle Mac," she said pertly. "I come all the way here from Greeley to drive for you—" She left the sentence dangling.

He was fingering his jaw as though it hurt, and he didn't answer her. She repeated in a louder voice, "I came out here to drive for you."

"I've already got somebody to drive for me."

"Where does that leave me?" She made a pouting grimace.

"Your aunt told you to come," he said shortly. "Then you two can figure it out. Here, girlie, sit down here."

Mrs. McKibben sat at the end of the table

with the coffee pot and stacked cups and saucers. Fabian was at her right and Eve at her left. Mr. McKibben was at the other end, with Stacy on his right and the man with the light, bushy hair and high cheekbones on his left. Fabian introduced him, "This is Vrest, Stacy. He's Mr. Mac's right hand."

Vrest added with a slow, ponderous smile in either a German or Swedish accent, "I am the nursemaid to the cow mamas and calves." A closer look told Stacy that he was older than she had thought at first sight. His hair wasn't blond but yellowed gray; his face was a myriad of sun wrinkles, and in his turkey-gobbler neck an Adam's apple bobbed up and down.

Stacy was a hearty eater for a girl who weighed only a hundred and five. And tonight she was hollow to her toes. She had meant to supplement her breakfast oatmeal by something more when she returned with the Novak car. But the judge waiting on the porch with his offer of a job had put all thought of food from her mind. She had been too shakily tense at noon to eat more than part of a doughnut with her tea.

So tonight she heaped her plate high and ate, though she scarcely knew what she was eating. The fried meat had dried out in the hour of waiting and required more chewing than Stacy, hungry and ill at ease, gave it.

She saw Mr. McKibben take boiled potatoes on his plate, mash them, and pour cream on them to make a purée. Wouldn't you think a wife whose husband was having tooth trouble would have prepared something special for him? Or, for that matter, wouldn't you think a man whose wife was absorbed in turning the Enos Starbrush house into a museum would show some interest in whether the old gilded frames fit her pictures?

It was a strange gathering around the big table that would easily have seated eight. You could have drawn a line through the middle and divided the six evenly into two factions: Mrs. McKibben, her co-worker Fabian, and her niece Eve at one end of the table; Mr. McKibben, his helper, and his girl driver at the other.

At Mrs. McKibben's end it was all museum talk. At Mr. McKibben's, all Herefords. Stacy was left out of both, although now and then Mr. McKibben turned to ask, "Getting enough to eat, girlie?"

The missus poured and passed the cups of coffee. Stacy took hers. She would have preferred milk, but she felt too unsure of herself even to mention it.

Mrs. McKibben was talking to her niece in a clear, distinct voice, "Of course, the Enos Starbrush home will be the big attraction Centennial Day. The mere fact that he was the founder—"

Her husband turned to Stacy. "His wagon wheel broke down when he was headed for the gold fields. So there he squatted, waiting for someone to come along with gumption enough to put it back together again."

Stacy laughed spontaneously. This was the kind of badinage that went on in her mother's family. Grandda O'Byrne loved to take sly digs at Gran's folks and their coming from the peat bogs in Ireland.

Mrs. McKibben went on talking—to Fabian this time, "Did you see about blowing up that old picture of the herd of Longhorns? It, too, has special significance since Enos Starbrush was the first to bring Longhorns to this part of the country."

Her husband enlightened Stacy on this, too. "You know why they called them Longhorns? Because they were long on horn, hide, and soupbones. You couldn't find enough meat on one to make a hamburger."

Stacy giggled further.

Eve asked, "Is that old organ you've got in the museum really the one your aunt or great-aunt Milly played on, Aunt Ev?"

"Yes, we traced it down, and we're having it repaired. I want to put a sign over it saying that it was used by the Songbird of Starbrush."

This time Mr. McKibben gave an explosive snort to Stacy. "Songbird! A lovesick old maid mewling on and on about unrequited love. 'What of My Shattered Heart?' 'Tell Me Not Good-bye.' Godamighty!"

Stacy threw back her head and laughed uproariously. It was the "What of My Shattered Heart?" that was so funny.

The very silence at the table stilled her laughter. She looked around and saw that everyone was intent on the food on his plate—everyone except Mrs. McKibben. Her lips were drawn thin; her eyes, cold and condemning, rested on Stacy.

So this wasn't family kidding. This wasn't for laughs. This was for real. And she had been lout enough to laugh.

She felt an all too familiar wave of nausea. *Oh, no—not now. Not here.* Her family always said that Stacy felt her griefs or upsets not in her heart or mind, but in her stomach. She gulped back the saliva and tried desperately to put her mind on something else. Perhaps she had turned pale green, for Mr. McKibben asked, "You tired, girlie?"

She stood up with a jerk and said in jerks, "If you don't mind—I'm going—to bed." She snatched up the purse at her feet. She even managed by clamping her jaws tight to *walk* up the stairs to the landing, go through the door, and close it after her. And then she *ran* the last half of the stairs and to the outsized bathroom, guided by the gray light from the windows.

The supper she had so hungrily gulped down, came up, and was flushed down the toilet. At last she steadied herself at the washbowl and again sloshed cold water on her face. She squirmed herself out of the green checked shirt, and washed it in the cold water with the bar of toilet soap.

If only she could take a warm bath. If only she had her Mexican bag into which she had so merrily wadded a couple of nightgowns. But Fabian had been too engrossed with Mrs. McKibben and the Songbird of Starbrush to bring it in or give a thought to what Stacy Belford had to sleep in.

She lost no time in stripping off her clothes, leaving on only her underpants. She spread out the blankets on the cot and crawled under them.

The wide double window in the room had not been curtained. Someone, maybe Eve, had tacked what looked like an old tablecloth across the lower half for privacy. A strong breeze, redolent of sage and cows, lifted and swirled it about. Stacy burrowed deeper into the pillow with no case on it, pulled the blankets under her chin, and shivered out, "I want to go home."

With aching clearness and dearness she pictured the shabby, untidy room she shared with Katie Rose. Her own lefthand drawer under the dotted-swiss skirt of the dressing table always stuck; Katie Rose kept telling her to rub the edges with wax, but Stacy never got around to it. The blob of spilled nail polish on the floor was something the shape of a sea horse. She thought longingly of the gentle and warm weight of Sidewinder as he curled up between her and Katie Rose.

The first large tear felt like a fly as it wended its way down her cheek and into her hair. Others came. She cried until she was salty and sodden with tears.

She would go home in the morning. When the bus went through Starbrush, Stacy Belford would be the first one on it. She traveled it in her mind and alighted at the downtown bus station. She wouldn't phone home but would take a southbound bus. She heard the click of their picket gate and felt herself fending off the exuberant Cully.

She was still awake when Eve came up, yawning and humming. She broke off both to say, "I brought up sheets and a pillow slip for you, if you want to get up and put them on."

Stacy pretended to be asleep. Not for worlds would she let Eve hear the tears in her voice. Eve went on humming and yawning.

A girl named Stacy Belford used to hum and sing, too, when she shucked off her clothes. But that girl had never been bruised by a woman greeting her with "We certainly don't need anyone else." That girl had never felt frostbitten by looks just because she laughed about the Starbrush wagon breaking down, about the horns, hide, and soupbones on a Longhorn, and even louder about a lovesick old maid writing "What of My Shattered Heart?"

Stacy's last waking thought was *Hurry, morning—oh, hurry—so I can get out of here*. She would get up early, long before anyone else was up, and drive the station wagon into Starbrush so as to be in plenty of time for the bus.

6

The bright sun in her eyes wakened Stacy the next morning. She sat up with a startled jerk and saw that the bed across the room was empty. She had overslept.

Her limbs were stiff and sore from her edge-of-the-seat driving yesterday. Again she thought longingly of a hot bath. But, no, as an unwelcome guest she had better make the best of the washbowl and cold water in the inadequate bathroom.

With her Mexican bag still in the car, she had no choice but to put on the same clothes she had taken off so hastily last night. The wraparound was mussed and dusty, but at least the drip-dry blouse was clean.

She felt the lump of car keys in her skirt pocket. Just eleven miles to Starbrush and the bus to Denver and Hubbell Street. Surely Fabian or Vrest or even Frozen-face could drive the station wagon back to the ranch. If Eve craved the job of chauffeuring, she was welcome to it.

Breakfast was over, she saw by the table

which Eve was clearing with a noisy clink of dishes. "I didn't mean to sleep so late," Stacy apologized.

"I'd have called you, but Uncle Mac said to let you get your sleep out."

Stacy stepped to the door and looked out through the screen. The collie didn't get up, but thumped her tail on the cement floor of the porch. "Where is everyone?"

"Aunt Eve had Fabe take her to look at a horsehair sofa. For the museum, natch."

Stacy remembered seeing a panel truck and also a Volkswagen parked under the big cottonwood last evening. The Volks was still there, and she asked, "Is the panel truck Fabian's?"

Whatever Eve said she said dramatically. "Are you crazy! Fabe's too poor to own a wheelbarrow. That panel is for the Centennial workers—mostly Fabian—to run around and cart things around in."

Stacy looked over the dining table. Only one piece of toast was left on it. Eve said, "I gave old Queenie the eggs and bacon that were left. There's coffee if you want to heat it up."

"I'd rather have milk if you have it."

"If we have it! We have enough milk around here to drown an elephant." She motioned to the kitchen table where sat several gallon glass jars with wide tops. "The more you drink, the less there'll be to skim cream off of."

Stacy used a glass of it to wash down the dry toast. "Where's Mr. McKibben this morning?"

"Where he always is. Out gloating over his

Prince Eric and all the little Erics and Ericas trotting along by their mamas. Oh yes, I'm to tell you to drive into Starbrush and get four salt blocks."

Stacy looked at her blankly, and Eve said, "For the critters to lick when they crave salt. You get them at the feedstore. They'll load them in for you."

Stacy turned away and took a long minute to rinse her glass out at the sink. She didn't want Eve to see the relief and joy in her face. This errand was heaven-sent. Now she wouldn't have to sneak off in the car to Starbrush to catch the bus.

"Four salt blocks," she repeated inanely.

"Just tell them at the feedstore they're for McKibben. Out here people get their money in lump sums when they sell off cattle or wheat or whatever. So then they go around and pay up their bills. About the only thing you need hard cash for is a bus ticket."

What a coincidence that Eve should have mentioned the very thing in Stacy's mind. She could hardly keep from asking, How much is the fare to Denver? Supposing she didn't have enough? She said, "We were at Pigeon Rock yesterday when the bus came through."

"It's a lot better bus now than the ones I used to come out here on. I rode for half fare for two years after I was past twelve—only I didn't tell Dad. He'd give me the seven twenty for full fare, and I'd feel so rich. I'd stuff myself on doughnuts at Pigeon Rock. The bus always stops at Ethel's Eat Shop in

Starbrush. You ought to taste her apple pie. I could live on sweet things."

Stacy was doing mental arithmetic. Seven twenty. She had the five-dollar bill Mother had tucked into her purse when she was leaving. And the two and a half dollars from the Novaks for baby-sitting. That was certainly shaving it close. She'd have thirty cents left, and Denver had recently raised the city bus fare to thirty cents.

She couldn't wait to leave. She opened the car door and turned on the motor. All the better for her departure that her one piece of luggage was still in the car. Again perching herself on the edge of the seat, she backed the long station wagon out from under the cottonwood, and headed it toward Starbrush—and Denver—and Hubbell Street.

She stopped for the barbed-wire gate that Fabian had handled so easily last evening. The gate consisted of about ten feet of four strands of wire stapled securely to the solid post in the ground and ending on the narrower post that was held in place by a loop of wire at the top and bottom of another grounded post. With much straining, she got the narrow, moveable post out of the wire loops that held it in place. She laid the gate to the side of the road, and drove through.

Coercing that slim post back in the wire loops was a hundredfold harder. She strained and tugged and shoved with every ounce of arm muscles. Breathless and desparing, she thought of leaving it open. After all, she wouldn't be coming back.

But white-faced cattle were grazing in the field, close enough so that she could hear them munching off mouthfuls of prairie grass. And this gate was to keep them there. So she tugged and tussled on until she closed it.

Driving down the road, she tried to think of some way to make her leave-taking seem less cowardly. Why couldn't she send Mr. McKibben word that she had telephoned home from Starbrush and found out that her mother was sick? Or that one of the littles had been hurt—

Oh, no, because saying it might make it come true. She remembered back to the time when she had planned at night that the next morning she would pretend her throat was sore so that she could stay home from school. And what happened? The next morning she had wakened with a bona fide raw and swollen throat.

She still hadn't thought of any excuse for being suddenly called home when she came to the caved-in sod church and made the turn. Nor when she crossed the railroad tracks by the filling station and was on the main street of Starbrush.

She might have parked the car at the feedstore with its sign about baby chicks and turks, but seeing the big, yellow sign Bus Stop, she pulled up beside a low building of simulated logs with ETHEL'S EAT SHOP painted above the door. She would ask inside what time the bus was due.

Ethel's Eat Shop was a one-room restaurant with a row of booths on one side of the room and a few square tables filling the space between them and the glass-covered pastry counter on the other. The watchful, green-smocked woman arranging luscious-looking pies under its glass, Stacy felt sure, was Ethel.

Two ranchers and a buxom woman with round cheeks were having coffee at one of the tables. A stooped man with thin, unkempt hair was sweeping the floor. They all looked at Stacy with friendly interest, and before she could ask about the bus, the round-cheeked woman lifted herself from her seat to get a better view out the window at the gray station wagon. She smiled at Stacy. "I guess you're the girl that's driving for McKibben. We heard he decided he'd rather have a girl driver."

The sweeper broke in, "I heard it, too. But I didn't know he'd hired himself Miss America to chauffeur him around." He pronounced it "show-foor" and chortled at his own wit.

One of the men at the table contributed, "I'll tell you this, miss—you'll never find a finer man than old Mac."

Stacy smiled back uncertainly. She hadn't thought about people in a small town knowing who she was. How could she account for her wanting to know what time the bus came through? But how account for her presence in an Eat Shop when she had no money to eat with, even though her stomach felt a great craving for the pies Ethel was displaying?

The man with the broom had more comments.

"Yeah, I don't blame old Mac for hiring a female. Must be a treat for him to have someone he can talk to and someone to answer him back. You wouldn't catch me buying groceries for a dame that put on a deaf-and-dumb act. Far as I know, nobody's collected any bets on the ice jam breaking up out there."

His remarks, which puzzled Stacy, seemed to embarrass the coffee drinkers. "Well, like I say, there's always two sides to—" the plump woman began, and Ethel broke in sharply from behind the counter, "That's about enough, Mr. Wise Guy. Finish your sweeping before the bus pulls in."

So the bus hadn't come yet. Stacy would wait outside so Ethel wouldn't ask her, "What can I do for you?" and Mr. Wise Guy wouldn't be having so much to say.

The door of the Eat Shop was opened by a rotund man in work-stained coveralls that barely buttoned over his middle. His easy-going smile included everyone in the restaurant, but his eyes rested on Stacy. "I guess you're the one I'm looking for. I guess you're Mac's new driver, eh?"

She nodded.

He was Lindstrom, he explained, of the Lindstrom Garage farther on down the street. And Mac had just phoned in from the ranch that he had sent his girl driver to town for salt blocks. But he wanted Lindstrom to take the car into the garage and work on the seat apparatus, so that when she pulled it forward, it wouldn't slide back.

"How did you know I was *here*?" she asked.

"Easy as falling off a log. I looked up and down the street and saw that long old buggy outside the Eat Shop here, and I told Mac where you were. And he said by damn, he bet Eve didn't give you enough breakfast, and for me to get on up here and tell Ethel to fix you up with whatever you wanted and chalk it up to him."

"I'll do just that," Ethel said.

"Mr. McKibben phoned you—about fixing the car seat?" Stacy breathed out. Then he remembered that she had had to perch herself on the very edge in order to reach the pedals. And he had worried about her not having enough breakfast.

"That's right. He told me to look out for you and look after you. So you sit right here and have whatever you can talk Ethel out of. I'll take the car down and work it over. I've got a couple of girl-crazy fellows working for me, and with a pretty girl like you there, I wouldn't get a tap of work out of either of them."

This seemed to call for a bright remark from the sweeper. "They're your kinfolks, Lindstrom, so maybe they come by it honest."

What a nice, untroubled smile the garageman had! "They're my kin all right. Sometimes I think I'm kin to all the brainless idiots in the country." And to Stacy, "While I'm about it, I'll have them load up your salt blocks at the feedstore."

She answered shakily, "Thanks, Mr. Lindstrom

—thanks a lot." *Thanks, Mr. Lindstrom—thanks a lot for changing my life.*

She was suddenly ashamed of her cowardly turning tail and running for home. Fine thing! She had answered an ad, claiming a strong character and tact. She had supposed, of course, that those traits were needed to deal with a fidgety, demanding boss instead of his inimical wife.

Her shoulders squared and her jaws tightened. *You, Mrs. Frozen-face, can go right on freezing me. And you, Mr. Medium Brown, with your marble-topped stand and stereopticons, and you, Eve, who'd like my job—the whole caboodle of you can go blow. I am Mr. McKibben's show-foor.*

"What would you like, dearie?" Ethel asked.

She answered promptly, "Apple pie with ice cream."

7

With the salt blocks, resembling huge and slightly dirty sugar cubes, in the back of the car, Stacy left town. It was easier driving with the seat adjusted to her size. She sang happily as she drove. She could sing without even knowing she was singing or what she was singing. This morning she went through a hymn and one of the Gay Nineties songs her mother played at the supper club.

And then she found herself crooning the one she and the boy, with challenging brown eyes and a grin on the bias, had danced to just a few nights ago in St. Jude's gym. The song was something about not giving all your love away, "Save some for a rainy day—"

She made her turn at the sod church that was no longer a church but only a landmark. Now the road ran along McKibben land. She hadn't followed the fence long when she saw Mr. McKibben and Vrest in the field bordering the road. They came toward her, shouting that they wanted one of the salt blocks at the windmill nearby. "Wait till we take the fence down—just wait now."

With hammer and pliers Vrest pulled out the staples that held the barbed-wire strands to the posts. The two men stood on the slack wires, holding them close to the ground, and Mr. McKibben impatiently motioned Stacy to drive over them. Not without trepidation, she maneuvered the car off the road, across a weed-grown ditch, and over the wires.

Vrest pounded them back in place. The two men rode with her across the plains to a windmill and the white-faced cows and calves grazing close by. Vrest unloaded one of the salt blocks. It was immediately surrounded by cows licking it with rough tongues.

Stacy got out too, picking her sandaled way between clumps of cacti. Wild roses grew close to the ground. Their gentle fragrance mingled with the ever-constant smell of cattle. She looked in surprise at a plant with dried-up, spiky leaves bearing a bloom of virginal, creamy-white waxen flowers. The stem was too tough to break off, and Vrest said, "Wait, I get out my knife."

He cut off the unbending stalk with its cluster of waxen flowers for her.

"Yucca. We call them soapweeds," Mr. McKibben said. "Yes, pretty. We get so used to walking around them, we don't even see them." He tilted his head for a glance at the sun high in the sky. "Not noon yet. You go on, girlie." He gestured in the direction she was to take. "You'll see the place as soon as you're over that first rise there."

She couldn't get back onto the road since Vrest had stapled the wires back on the fence, so she drove on over the prairie sod. She saw the white buildings and the big cottonwood before she had gone far. But she had to follow a winding gully slowly and anxiously until she found a place she decided was safe enough to guide the heavy car across.

At home she stopped in the shade of the cottonwood, feeling a confidence in herself that she had not known when she left earlier this morning. She carried her stiff stalk of white blossoms and her striped Mexican bag into the house. The big room was empty, and she stepped to the kitchen doorway.

Eve sat on a high stool. She was putting her hair up on curlers and listening with a faraway look on her face to a blues record on her portable player. She was evidently not expecting to see Stacy, for her feet dropped from the rung of the stool and she stared at her unbelievingly. "You! You came back. I never thought—I thought sure you'd—" She checked herself abruptly.

Stacy stared back at her for a full half minute. So all Eve's talk about the bus and the price of the ticket to Denver hadn't been coincidence after all.

Stacy said with biting sarcasm, "I'm sorry to disappoint you, Eve. But it so happens that Judge McKibben hired me to drive for his father. It so happens that Mr. McKibben wants me. So whether you like me or not, I'm going to stay."

She started toward the stairs. Eve slid off the stool and caught her arm. "Now look, you don't have to get so feisty about it. I haven't got a darn thing against you. It's just that Aunt Evvy said I was to drive for Uncle Mac because he couldn't get along with Fabe. It's just that now I'll be stuck here in the house with cooking and all that because Aunt Ev is running her legs off with that sappy Starbrush Centennial—"

"You can always go home if you don't like it here."

"That's what you think." She made a grimace of woe. "Dad and my stepmother just count the days till school's out so they can get rid of me. I wanted to stay in Greeley this summer because I'm in with a real groovy bunch. But the minute Aunt Evvy phoned and said come, they couldn't say good-bye quick enough."

Eve turned her head and the rapt expression came back. She tilted her head toward the record player. "Listen. This is the part that really shakes me."

Stacy listened to a man's voice pleading for someone to take his hand and wander down the road with him to Nowhere Land. "It shakes me, too," Stacy admitted honestly.

The spleen came back to Eve's voice, "If there's anything I loathe and despise it's cooking and washing dishes and tending to all the milk. And milk buckets—such a lovely cow-and-manurey smell!—and all those jars, and skimming cream—Gah! Did you ever wash milky things? They turn the water slimy if you use soap, and how can you get them clean if you don't?"

Stacy said, "I'm not much good at housework, but I'll help when I'm not driving Mr. McKibben around. I got my bag out of the car, so I can change clothes. Fabian forgot to bring it in last night."

"Forgot?" That meaningful roll of eyes and shrug. "Accidentally on purpose, he forgot. He didn't think you'd stay either."

Fresh anger sizzled through Stacy. So Fabian too had counted on her taking the bus back to Denver and hadn't thought it worthwhile to unload her bag.

She was still standing there, the bag at her feet, quite forgetting that she wanted to change her clothes, when the two searchers for antiques returned. Mrs. McKibben came into the house. Perhaps she too was surprised to see the unwelcome guest still there, but she gave no sign. She answered Eve's "Did you get the hairy old sofa?" with "No, we found it wasn't worth bringing home."

Stacy stepped out the door. She didn't see Fabian, but she followed the sound of splashing water to the side of the house. There was an outdoor faucet over a weathered washstand with a basin and soap dish. Fabian was running the water and washing his hands.

He smiled at Stacy and said of the yucca blossom she held, "It still amazes me that such a dried-up, ugly plant can produce such a lovely—almost sacred flower. Notice how each blossom looks like an ivory chalice?"

She didn't answer that, but parted her thinned lips on a derisive laugh. "You cover your disappointment better than Eve."

"Disappointment?"

"At seeing that I'm still here. Oh, don't pretend you didn't want me to leave too. Don't pretend that you *forgot* to bring my bag in out of the car. You left it there on purpose."

"That's right," he agreed. "I didn't know whether you could take all you had to take out here or not. So I just thought, in case you couldn't, I'd make it easy for you to duck out."

"Well, break down and cry. Because I'm not ducking out whether you want me to or not."

His voice was reasoning, gentle. "I don't want you to, Stacy. But I could see last night how much it hurt you to have Mrs. Mac giving you the cold shoulder."

"Why does she hate me so?"

"It isn't *you* she hates, young'un. She'd hate the queen of England if Mr. Mac brought her in and called her girlie. You'll just have to get used to those two. To their not talking to each other—"

"You mean they don't *speak* to each other?" Her words came in slow wonder, "Of course—I mean, that's why nothing seemed right last night—only I didn't realize—"

"Didn't you realize they talk *at* each other? You'll learn that when she speaks quite clearly and distinctly to Eve or you or me, her remarks are aimed at *him*. And all his snide remarks to you last night about Enos Starbrush and poor Milly were meant for *her*."

"So that's what the fellow with the broom was talking about—I stopped at Ethel's Eat Shop. He was going on about Mr. McKibben hiring a female so he could talk to her and she would answer back. And he said something about bets on when the ice jam would break."

"Yes, the whole country wonders how much longer it'll go on."

"I can't imagine a married couple not speaking. How long have they been like that? What did they get so mad at each other about?"

"Over a year ago. And about Prince Eric and the unfinished upstairs. About his going up to a stock show in Denver and getting so carried away that he paid a huge price for the Prince when she was counting on using the money for a guest room and bath."

"So that's how it got nipped in the bud. Gosh and golly!"

Fabian took off his glasses. "Hold them a minute, will you?" He splashed water over his face, fumbled a paper towel out of the bottom of the washstand, and dried it. "It's really the old triangle," he went on as he took back his glasses. "Only instead of Mrs. Mac being jealous of another woman in her husband's life, she's jealous of his Herefords—and especially Prince Eric. I have a feeling she's getting back at him—I mean all her dedicated resurrecting old great-grandpappy Enos Starbrush is—"

"And Milly."

He chuckled. "Oh, yes, Milly the Songbird of Starbrush. And you didn't help your cause any by laughing like a hyena at Mr. Mac calling her a lovesick old maid."

"But it was funny—that about 'What of My Shattered Heart?' A heart doesn't really shatter, does it, Fabian?"

"Not permanently. The heart's made of pretty tough gristle, so all the little shatters and splinters gradually get glued together again."

"Are you talking from experience?"

She liked his small, tucked-in, self-deprecating smile. "Remember, I'm an old man of twenty-seven? Nobody can go that long without a shatter. To get back to Mrs. Mac. You've read all these fairy stories about—Oh, that's right. You don't read."

"But I've had them read to me. So what about them?"

"About how all the fairies are always asked to the christening of a new little princess. And one brings beauty, and another a happy disposition, and maybe another a long life. But none of them brings what seems to me the most priceless gift—a sense of humor. That's what you have to remember about Mrs. Mac. She doesn't have a lick of one.

If she had, she could laugh about 'What of My Shattered Heart?' and she'd be happier, and so would everyone around her. Eve got passed up on the sense of humor, too."

"I don't know how to take Eve. She's different from any girl I know."

"Just take anything she says—or does—with a grain of salt, and you'll get along."

"Do I have a sense of humor, Fabian?"

He gave her his rare smile that robbed his face of its schoolteacher look. "Yes, I'd say *all* the good fairies made it to your christening."

Stacy's heart warmed and lifted. He was nice to talk to. She looked down at her stalk of flowers. Yes, each separate floweret was like a candleholder or a chalice. "I saw wild roses, too," she said.

"They're thick as pink polka dots near the Rattlesnake—creek, that is—where my ducks are."

"I'd like to see them. I'd like to see your ducks."

"Yes, you must see my Lauderbach family."

Eve came out the kitchen door and clanged the dinner bell.

Mr. McKibben and Vrest made a somewhat dramatic entrance into the room where the table was set. Vrest was holding aloft a folded sheet of paper, and he was laughing, although it sounded as though he were trying to cough up something stuck in his throat. "Here is what we found stuck on a salt block. It is a letter, but we don't think it is for Mac or me because neither one of us is a beautiful bundle." His "we" was *ve*, and his "think," *tink*.

Eve plopped a huge bowl of cole slaw on the table and said, "Let's see," and grabbed the paper out of his hand. She said, "I wish you'd listen!" and read aloud:

"Beautiful bundle:

We've been framed. Old Fabe Brown outfoxed us yesterday. Our boss outfoxed us this morning by keeping you away from the garage where we slave. But we saw you as you drove out of town. We adore you.

Love and kisses,
Wild Bill Hickok
Enrico Caruso"

Everybody laughed, Stacy as joyfully as any. Vrest predicted, "You'll have your hands full with those two lady-killers." Eve said, "It's because you're new, Stacy. They give every new girl a mad rush."

Everybody laughed, except Mrs. McKibben. Like Queen Victoria she was *not* amused.

Again the invisible dividing line at the table. Again Eve set down a platter of meat, dried and curled at the edges. Mr. McKibben studied it, the hard rolls, and the cole slaw. He put one hand up to gently finger his cheek and turned to Stacy. "Girlie, would you go into the kitchen and boil me a couple of medium-soft eggs?"

Eve remarked as Stacy pushed back her chair, "There's no way you can time them. The kitchen clock is all screw-gee, and this one on the wall has stopped."

Mrs. McKibben added in the clear, distinct

voice that Fabian said she used when her remark was meant for her husband, "It stopped months ago. Whenever anything gets out of order in the house, it stays out of order. The fences and windmills and cattle shed are kept in A-one repair, of course. But then Herefords are far more important around here than humans."

Stacy said, "I don't need a clock to time eggs." If it hadn't been for Mrs. McKibben's forbidding presence, she would have explained that at the Belford home, two stanzas of "Rose of Tralee" did for the morning oatmeal and only one for medium-soft eggs.

She put the eggs on and brought them to a boil. She turned the butane gas down to low under them and began to hum under her breath. But the words that formed in her mind were not "The pale moon was rising above the green mountain—" They were "I don't give a hoot if Frozen-face hates me—"

8

In the days that followed, Stacy was to say that to herself again and again, "I don't give a hoot whether she hates me or not." They were busy days of driving Mr. McKibben to neighboring ranches while he lined up a crew for his alfalfa cutting and on trips to Starbrush to get mower blades sharpened.

She was to say it aloud to Fabian while he freshened up at the outdoor faucet and washstand, "Okay, so I'm the fly in her butter. If she thinks I care, she's crazy."

But she did care. Mrs. McKibben's cool politeness nagged at her. She was used to liking everyone and being liked in return. "You know, Fabian, I can't remember anyone not liking me before—ever."

"No, I don't imagine you can. Don't let it worry you. Psychologists claim that one isn't an adult as long as he expects or craves everyone's liking him."

"Wouldn't it bother you if somebody didn't?"

"I'd be bothered plenty if it did. You've noticed

how your Mr. Mac has no use for me. It's because I'm part of all this Starbrush celebration and he has no use for that." He gave his low rumble of chuckle. "And that's because the missus keeps rubbing his nose in the exemplary and unsurpassed Starbrushes."

Yes, Stacy had noticed the belittling snort Mr. McKibben gave whenever Fabian made a comment.

Stacy had been there a week when Mr. McKibben sent her into Elmore to pick up a document for him at the land office. Elmore was the county seat. It was twice the size of Starbrush and over twice the distance from the McKibben ranch. Eve went with her to show her the way.

The business tended to, they were having Cokes at the drugstore fountain when Stacy took from her purse her five-dollar bill to pay for them. Eve said, "Hey, lend me enough for a bottle of shampoo, and I'll pay you back real soon."

She returned to the fountain and Stacy with several packages. "I got some Capri Copper. I never dreamed I'd find it here. You can help me put it on. And I had to get these plastic gloves for the job." She also had the shampoo she had started out to buy, and a nickel and two pennies left from Stacy's five dollars. "It's the most gorgeous auburn, and I've just been dying to—whatta you know!—I've just been dying to dye."

That evening Stacy helped her through the smelly and painstaking process that turned Eve from a brunette to a copperish redhead.

A few days later Stacy saw Fabian's ducks. It came about through Mrs. McKibben's clearing the bread box of stale bread and pastries and saying to Eve, "You can drive my Volks over to the Brown place with some of this for Fabian's ducks."

Every few days Mrs. McKibben left the Starbrush museum to fare on its own while she stayed home and turned housewife and ranch woman. She was a dynamo of energy, and so efficient that she could accurately dovetail her breadmaking, garden work, churning, looking over chickens and coops, and cooking enough ahead to last for days. She was, as her son had said, an excellent cook when she wanted to be.

She was an early-to-bed, early-to-rise person and the antithesis of Stacy's mother. Even when Mother wasn't playing the piano till after midnight at the supper club, she would still stay up late.

And Mrs. McKibben emerged from her room each morning, fully dressed, well combed, and with even a trace of rouge on cheeks that were plump but sallow. She tied on a starched apron, with appliquéd pockets in the shape of an apple or tulip, before starting breakfast.

The Belfords' mother came into the kitchen each morning heavy-eyed, fastening a robe on over her nightgown. One of the children would pull the robe's rumpled collar out for her. Her last night's lipstick would be smeared in spite of her half-hearted rinsing of her face. The pompadour effect would still show in her red hair in spite of her running a comb through it. She'd give them all a sleepy smile and ask on a yawn, "Isn't the coffee ready yet?" She always said that her red blood corpuscles didn't connect until her second cup of coffee.

Mother too was a dynamo of energy, but her energy was impulsive—or inspired. In the middle of the afternoon she might suddenly decide that the scuffed floor of their front porch needed painting. And just as suddenly she'd set to work. Stacy had known her to come home from her Gay Nineties club at two in the morning and decide to wash the dinette curtains. Then, having a washer full of soapy water, she'd gather up more things to thrust in.

But, try as she might, Stacy couldn't imagine her mother holding a grudge—and her tongue—for over a year.

This day of the bread-box cleaning, Stacy ran down to the cowsheds to ask Mr. McKibben if he needed her to drive. If not, she'd like to go over to the Brown place with Eve to see Fabian's ducks.

"Fabian's ducks!" he snorted with the same disgust as though he were saying, "Fabian's dolls!" He added, "Go ahead—go ahead. We're moving Prince Eric up to the home pasture."

The house on the Brown place was indeed brown, and snuggled low under the vines that covered its front. Fabian was home. He left the room he had made into a workshop and walked to the pond with Eve and Stacy. Their bread was tossed on the water and gobbled up by the fully feathered ducks and by others whose down had not yet given way to feathers.

Fabian said in loud reproach, "Shame on you, Mrs. Lauderbach, for being so hoggish."

A white duck lifted her head and quacked back angrily. He scolded on, "A fine grandma and great-grandma you are—taking bread out of your little ones' mouths."

This time she ruffled her feathers and took a few steps toward him, quacking even more vehemently.

"What's she saying?" Stacy asked.

"She's telling me to mind my own business—that she knows more about raising a duck family than I do."

On the ride home Eve said, "Doesn't poor old Fabe just break your heart? He's so poor, and he's had to slave to educate himself. He was hired to organize the Centennial and get publicity for it. But what happens? He's at everybody's beck and call. All those fool women that are supposed to be restoring the Starbrush house are on his neck night and day."

"He seems to like gathering up old relics and fixing them."

"He pretends he likes it because he needs the pay so's he can buy a camper to live in this year to save room rent while he finishes getting that high-up degree."

Stacy got out to open the gate between the Brown acreage and the road. This too was one of the tight ones that took a straining of arm muscles. Eve resumed when Stacy dropped down in the seat beside her, puffing for breath, "And poor old Fabe has always been neglected and unloved and—"

"He said his parents were killed in Mexico when he was five or six."

"Yes, but why weren't they home taking care of him instead of poking around in ruins down there? And the way his selfish old gadabout grandma griped to him and everybody else about what a burden he was. And how she hated to be tied down. Well, he didn't tie her down long. By the time he was twelve or thirteen, she left him on his own all summer while she went sailing off in her car to heaven knows where."

"I guess that's why he wanted ducks—because he was lonely," Stacy mused.

"A lot his grandmother cared whether he was lonely or not. A lot she cares now whether he ever gets a square meal or not. Aunt Ev insists on his coming there for lunch and dinner—only out here it's dinner and supper. He ought to come for breakfast, too. He says he has to eat the duck eggs because he can't sell them."

Stacy paid Eve's aunt sincere tribute. "That's awfully good of her to have him there for meals."

"Yes. Well, to tell the truth, she likes to have

him on hand to help her run down horsehair sofas and such for the Starbrush museum."

Stacy saw Prince Eric that same afternoon. Mr. McKibben was leading him past the house, and he called her to come out. So this was the bone of contention between McKibben husband and wife. Yet it didn't seem right to even use the word *bone* about Prince Eric when solid flesh and glistening red and brushed hide covered every one of his. He turned his head, and his round pale eyes rested with boredom on Stacy.

His owner ran a loving hand over the tight white curls on the Prince's forehead. The white on the bull's face ran down his paunchy breast and belly.

"I'm putting him out here in the home field. Did you ever see a handsomer critter?"

"No, I never did. He looks like he weighs a lot." She thought, but didn't say, that unlike a Longhorn he would supply a lot of hamburgers.

"Twenty-one hundred on the hoof. Feel his solid flesh."

She stuck a tentative finger in the firm region of his ribs. The prince deigned to give her another bored look out of bulging pale eyes.

Mr. McKibben tugged gently at the white braided halter, and he and his prize bull went on. Stacy glanced at the garden where Mrs. McKibben was using a hoe to direct a flow of water along the rows. How she must hate the sight of Prince Eric!

In the kitchen, Eve was noisily stirring up Kool-ade. "Well, were you ecstatic at the sight of Eric the Great, and did you oh and ah enough over him?" She poured Stacy a glass of the red liquid and added, "Honestly, it'd only be poetic justice if lightning struck that big hunk of suet he's so nuts about."

"Eve! That's a terrible thing to say."

"Uncle Mac is a terrible man. You don't know him the way I do. Or how poor old Aunt Ev planned and dreamed for years of making that upstairs into a guest room with a nice bath. She had the bedroom wallpaper all picked out—pale blue with white daisies. And she was braiding a blue and white rug for the bath. Some yokel plumber put in that silly washbowl and toilet up there years ago, and she counted on going ahead with it when Uncle Mac took up his yearling heifers and sold them."

"Fabian told me about it."

"Did he tell you that he didn't bring a dollar home to her? Instead—thrill-thrill!—he brings home the prince. I don't blame her for not speaking one solitary word to him from that day to this, or for moving his clothes out of her bedroom onto that closed-in porch one."

Stacy felt her sympathies veer toward the woman whose rosy plans for a guest room and bath upstairs had been nipped in the bud by the heavy chunk that was Prince Eric. She didn't realize then that Eve's recital of a story depended entirely on her own mood at the moment of telling.

The very next day Eve slanted her story differently.

Stacy returned at noon from driving Mr. McKibben on a tour of fields, windmills, and alfalfa stacks. His wife's car had driven in just ahead of them. She had evidently asked a guest to noonday dinner, for not only did she and Fabian get out and go into the house, but also a small balding man in a very loud sport shirt.

"That's the prancy little pipsqueak that trains the school band," Mr. McKibben said.

Stacy and he got out and stood for a moment in the cooling shade of the cottonwood. The sound of one of Eve's blues records reached out to them. They heard it clicked off right in the middle of a loud and long-drawn "ba-ay-by." In another moment Mrs. McKibben came out the kitchen door, holding a bread pan by a pot holder. She stepped a few feet from the porch and gave an angry fling of its contents to the ground. These turned out to be burnt and smoking rolls that bounced on the ground and dismayed the chickens, who came running toward them and then stopped short.

Stacy went into the kitchen to ask if she could help. Eve waited until her aunt carried in a plate of sliced bread to the table in the big room, and then she exploded in a whisper that was more of a hiss, "Will someone tell me one thing? Just one thing? How poor old Uncle Mac can live with that woman. Just show me any other man that'd put up with her treating him like dirt, and not even speaking to him, or boiling him an egg—"

"But you said he spent their money on Prince Eric when—"

"Sure, he bought Prince Eric. To build up his herd. A purebred bull is worth its weight in gold to a cattleman. He saw a chance to get him for a good price; so why let a chance of a lifetime slip by just because she wanted wallpaper with daisies on it? She thinks everyone should kowtow to her just because she has Starbrush blood in her veins—"

"But it's too bad she couldn't go ahead on the bedroom and bath upstairs."

"She could if she wanted to—don't think she couldn't. She just leaves it that way to act like a martyr. She could at least put the braided rug in the bathroom."

Her tirade broke off as Fabian came into the kitchen.

Three days later Fabian ceased to be "Poor old Fabe."

He came out from the Starbrush museum in midafternoon for some Battenberg curtains Mrs. McKibben wanted for the parlor windows in the Starbrush house.

"Eve, I stopped in at the post office, and there was a package there for you."

"Oh, it's come. That's the new 'Embers Light Fires' album. Where is it?"

"It's still at the post office."

"Why didn't you bring it out?"

"It came C.O.D., so there was four dollars and thirty-seven cents worth of why."

"You could have paid for it, and I'd have paid you back."

He made no answer to that, but went out the door with the Battenberg curtains.

Eve looked after him with head shakings and tight lips. "There goes the great scholar, the intellectual," she said bitterly, "with a soul as small as a pea. Everybody feels sorry for his hardworking grandmother and her getting stuck with such a selfish, stuck-up, unfeeling monster. No wonder she takes off about the time he's due to come home. He wouldn't lift a finger for anyone. It wouldn't have hurt him to get my album for me."

Stacy, thinking of the seven cents she had got back from her five dollars, wondered if Fabian might not have had the same experience. Stacy had said to her once, "I'm going in to Starbrush, and I'm broke, and I thought maybe you could pay me back."

That shrug of Eve's that was like an exclamation point. "How can I pay you back when Aunt Evvy hasn't paid me one cent for being a flunkey —not yet. What do you need money for? You can always charge anything to McKibbens."

The next week when Katie Rose wrote to Stacy and enclosed six dollars she owed her in the letter, Stacy said nothing of it to Eve.

Eve had widened her eyes in horror when Stacy first told her about her family. "*Five* brothers and sisters! Oh, no. If I had all those I'd buy a rope and look for the first rafter to hang myself on."

"Why?"

"Oh, because"—a wincing grimace—"I can't bear people pressing against me."

"I'm abnormal," Stacy said gravely. "And all my family are. I'm always ashamed to confess it."

"How are you abnormal?"

"I like my family. And we all like each other. But don't tell anybody."

"Stop pulling my leg," Eve said crossly.

On a chilly, wet night in late June, Eve sat up in her bed reading aloud parts of her letter from a boy named Fallico. Poor Fallico, she told Stacy, was on probation for smoking pot.

Stacy had driven Mr. McKibben to a cattlemen's meeting at Elmore that afternoon. They had returned after a heavy downpour. Stretches of the dirt road had been so much wet gumbo to drive through. It was Stacy's first experience in handling a car that slithered and skidded—and a nerve-wracking experience it was, with Mr. McKibben barking at her, "Keep your foot off the brake. Worst thing you can do. Don't touch the brake."

So Stacy listened, her eyes blinking heavily, as Eve went on, "Fallico wants me to run off to California with him—you know, take the road to nowhere together. He needs love and understanding and a hand to hold to—and so do I—and we could find ourselves—"

"You'd find yourselves in a large-sized mess."

"Oh sure, sure. It's all right for you to make fun of people like us that are unwanted and lost in a fog. You've got a swell big family that loves you—"

No mention of buying a rope and hunting a rafter now.

"—and you've got a mother that loves you," Eve lamented on, "and thinks enough of you to phone. You don't see that woman that married my father phoning me, do you?"

"Mom's the kind that phones to somebody when she misses them." Stacy yawned widely. "Ben's always raising Cain about the phone bills."

Mother the impulsive often called about four o'clock, which was tea time at the Belfords' on Hubbell. "Stacy, love, I'm just cutting the brown bread, and it doesn't seem right without you here grabbing for the crust." (Every morning in the world Mother baked a round, lumpy loaf of Irish soda bread.)

"I'll grab when I come home."

"Oh, yes, Stacy, and a fellow named Pete has been phoning you. He says he met you at the St. Jude's dance."

"Pete? Pete? Oh, yes, the guitar player in the Sing Out." But that all seemed like another world and that Stacy, light-hearted in her Junior escort dress, like some other girl.

"Are you all right, my dear own? Are they good to you out there?"

"Don't be silly, Mom. Of course, they are."

Even when Mrs. McKibben was not within listening distance, Stacy couldn't bring herself to say, "You've no idea how awful it is to sit at the table with someone who doesn't like you. It chills my soul."

She still felt waves of homesickness. But not since that first night of weariness, hurt, nausea, and sobs had she any desire to run home to mother. She, Stacy, had got herself into this situation, and she, Stacy, must make the best of it.

From her mussed bed, Eve grumbled on, "You lack understanding because life has never kicked you around. Not the way it has some of us."

Stacy made no answer. She was sound asleep.

But even though she learned to take Eve's exaggerations and changes of mood not with the *grain* of salt Fabian advised but with a good-sized spoonful, Stacy liked her. She was appealing and disarming and fun to be around. Whenever the men were in the fields and Mrs. McKibben and Fabian were out hunting antiques, Eve would say, "You can take a bath first if you don't use up all the hot water."

So Stacy would ration her water in the unduly long and narrow tub in the downstairs bath.

And Eve was fun to giggle with. Like the morning when her curler dropped into the skillet where the sausages were frying. The girls were helping Mrs. McKibben with her breakfast-getting, and it was when Eve bent over the skillet to turn the sausages that one of her curlers dropped in and, because it was the same size as those plump, sizzling links, blended beautifully.

The two laughed hilariously, but Eve's aunt removed it and—again like Queen Victoria—was not amused.

"I just wish Fabe was here so I could put it on his plate," Eve said.

9

On the first day of July, Stacy came downstairs dressed in a sleeveless cream-colored linen with a wide green belt and her green sandals. She hadn't worn the sandals after that first day when she found that cacti were not kind to unprotected feet.

She felt festive and eager. This morning she was driving Mr. McKibben to an auction sale at the Dormeir ranch twenty-seven miles away. For several weeks he and Vrest had been studying the handbill which told of the horses, cows, calves, pigs, and poultry that would be put under the gavel and go to the highest bidder.

Mr. McKibben announced to everyone at the breakfast table, "Nothing there I want to buy. I'm just going to see what yearling Herefords are bringing."

Mrs. McKibben also announced to the table but in that distinct voice which Stacy, even as Fabian, knew was meant for her husband's ears, "An auction sale out here is just a chance for men to get away from work for a day. And for women to get together and gossip, and young people to make eyes at each other."

Vrest put in on his throat-catching laugh, "And for everybody to eat all they can stuff down for nothing." ("Notting," he pronounced it.)

Stacy tied a green ribbon around her hair in front of the kitchen mirror. She hated to think of Eve being left at home alone all day, for Fabian and Mrs. McKibben were again setting forth in search of a sofa to go in the Enos Starbrush museum.

"Eve, let me help with the dishes so you can come to the sale with us. It'll be fun."

"It's not my idea of fun." Eve gave a bellowing imitation of an auctioneer. " 'Going—going—*gone*!' And thousands of hoodlum kids tearing around and all but knocking you down. Besides Uncle Mac doesn't dote on me the way he does on you. And *besides*"—the dramatic roll of eyes—"I'm expecting a phone call and, who knows? I might be on the road to nowhere by the time you and the horsehair-sofa hunters come back."

The handbill stated that the sale would start promptly at nine. But Mr. McKibben, instead of leaving promptly, fidgeted restlessly about. It wasn't until his wife drove off with Fabian that he sprang into action. He ordered Stacy to back the station wagon up close to the implement shed. He and Vrest lost no time in pushing out a stock trailer and fastening it on.

"You never know what they might be giving away," he said with a boyish wink at Stacy.

But when she stopped at the McKibben gate, he didn't climb out promptly to open it, but sat a thoughtful moment before he said, "Now, girlie, don't let me get carried away. I haven't got room for more than four more heifers, and I can't afford more than that. In fact, I'll have to buy the four on credit, so don't let me bid on one hoof more."

"I'll drag you away by main force when you've got your four," she promised.

He got out and opened the gate. She thought back to her first morning on the plains when she was bent on running home and had struggled so desperately with this same gate. Her arm muscles had strengthened since then.

Three weeks. Her days had fallen into a certain pattern. At sunup, she would be wakened by the bang of the door under the window and her bed. That would be Mr. McKibben. Simultaneously another door would slam, which meant that Vrest was leaving the bunkhouse. It was as though the same inner alarm clock sounded at the same time for each man.

She would hear the clink of milk buckets. By now she didn't need to glance out the window to know that Mr. McKibben, who had left the kitchen with two buckets, was handing one to Vrest.

With a bound she would get out of bed, her cheeks pink from the breeze that blew over her while she slept. By now she had ceased to notice the ever-present cow smell the breeze carried.

Part of the pattern of her days was the brief

time of talking to Fabian there on the shady side of the house while he washed for the noonday meal. "I'm the little girl who isn't here, Fabian. Your Mrs. Mac can barely see me."

"She's not a happy woman this summer."

"Pardon me while I sob for her. Why isn't she happy when she enjoys making everyone else unhappy?"

"I wonder if she does. I wonder if she isn't wishing the ice jam between her and Mr. Mac would break."

"There's no law against her breaking it, is there? All she has to do is to say she's sorry she's been such an iceberg."

"Sounds easy, but pride—pride. Isn't it one of the seven deadly sins? And then this Centennial celebration is her baby, and at the committee meeting last night—"

"I don't want to hear about the Centennial. I'm so sick of it. I mean *sick*. It just turns my stomach."

Another day she said, "The evenings are so long and empty out here, Fabian."

"I suppose you miss all that kicking up of heels you had in Denver."

"What do *you* do in the evening?"

"I fiddle-faddle in the workshop, or turn on the hi-fi and read. Sometimes watch TV. Do you ever see Marcia Mills's Special Events program?"

"Not if I can help it."

"She puts on a good show," he defended. "I went to the university with her. And I'm hoping

I can lure her out to Starbrush to cover the Centennial."

"Please, Fabian, not the Centennial again."

Another noontime Fabian said, "I saw your girl-hungry jokers last evening. The ones who adore you."

"Oh, yeah! Then why couldn't they phone or use up a little gas coming out?"

"There's a reason. I tried to tell you what happened at that Centennial meeting, but you didn't want to hear about it."

"I still don't want to hear it. And if the jokers are mixed up in the Centennial, I'd rather swivel on the vine than get mixed up with them."

It was Eve who told Stacy, "Those goofballs that signed Wild Bill Hickok and Enrico Caruso really are named Bill and Enrico. The Lindstroms are Swedes, and why a Swede would name a kid Enrico I wish I knew. And Bill and Enrico are second cousins or something."

This morning as she drove to the Dormeir auction, she saw Mr. McKibben glance at the pencil-like shadows of the fence posts along the road. Stacy too had learned to gauge time by the shadows cast by them, by buildings, and by the cottonwood tree that sheltered the station wagon.

She hazarded, "About ten, isn't it?"

He nodded. "But they'll auction off the little stuff first—chickens, pigs, and lambs. They won't get to the cows and heifers till after dinner."

"I've never been to an auction before. I can't

wait to get there." They smiled happily at each other.

As a boss, he was not an easy one. He was impatient, explosive, often unreasonable. She would be driving along at a good clip when he would suddenly bellow, "Whoa—whoa! Stop here." He always urged her to go faster than the speed limit. "I hate poking along." He'd order her to cut across fields so that he could check on the hay on a river bottom.

She would drive across the prairie, lurching over weed-grown stubble and prairie-dog holes, with cacti crunching under the wheels. He'd motion her to cross Rattlesnake Creek after a heavy rain when the water ran hub-deep, and its sandy bottom was full of holes.

The car by now was not an inanimate bit of machinery to Stacy, but more of a faithful, willing, and even eager friend. So that when it creaked and strained or its bottom scraped on the earth, she winced in sympathy as though it were a living body and not metal.

Often when she'd get back on solid road, her foot would be shaking on the pedal and the palms of her hands wet with perspiration on the wheel.

An irascible and roguish man, but she loved Mr. McKibben.

"Turn up there where those other cars are turning," he directed her this midmorning. And a few minutes later, "There's the Dormeir place. Big crowd. Look at the cars parked all around. Look at them streaking in from all directions."

"Don't forget your contraption," she reminded him.

His new partial plate still bothered him. He removed it often, and Stacy had to remind him to put it back when they neared their destination. He now turned his head from her, ducked it low, and came up muttering, "Don't think I'll ever get used to the cussed thing."

By now cars were ahead of the station wagon and behind it. A few of them passed, the passengers waving a greeting as they did. And then one car came alongside them. But it didn't whizz past. It was a very old jeep, so that its two occupants were sitting much higher than the passengers in the McKibben car.

The thin gangling boy, who was driving, had draped his height around the wheel. His companion was shorter, and he had more meat on his bones. His hair and his beard, in the embryo stage, were darker and had more body than those of his companion, which were blowing like thistledown in the wind.

The more substantial one was kneeling on the seat, stretching out his arms toward Stacy with a "Come to me" gesture, breaking the movement now and then to throw impassioned kisses at her.

The thin one at the wheel, looking for all the world like a whiskered banshee, took off his glasses and waved them at Stacy with a grin that was far more shy than his seatmate's.

"Watch where you're going, you brainless idiot," Mr. McKibben thundered out at him. And then, "Godamighty, girlie, there they are—the quiz kids, the lover boys from Lindstrom's garage." He gave a loud snorting guffaw. "I wish Vrest was here to see their crazy monkeyshines."

Stacy laughed in sheer excitement and delight.

10

In the small traffic jam, and with Stacy's hunting a space for their long car among all the ones parked haphazardly around the Dormeir ranch buildings, she was separated from the jeep and the exuberant two.

Even here at the auction there were reminders of the coming Centennial Day. Men climbing out of cars were growing moustaches and beards while windshields or back windows bore stickers:

COME TO THE
STARBRUSH CENTENNIAL
AUGUST 23

As Stacy and Mr. McKibben made their way toward the corrals, a pig's indignant squeal rent the air. "Still selling and loading up pigs," he commented.

Suddenly the two jeep passengers blocked Stacy's path. The tall boy stood with a sober face, his glasses dropped halfway down his nose, but the medium-sized one fell on his knees, and grasped the hem of Stacy's cream-colored linen and cried out in an anguished voice, "How could you desert me and all our poor little children to go off with that toothbrush salesman?"

The ham in Stacy couldn't help responding, "I know I shouldn't ought to have, but gee, he smelled so nice."

Folks around them stopped and looked on with appreciative smiles and chuckles. Evidently the jokers were well known. The pleader got to his feet and threw his arms around her, crying out lustily, "All is forgiven. Come back, come back."

Each of the boys took an arm and walked beside her. "Just call me Enrico Caruso," the shorter one said. "And my pal here answers to Wild Bill."

Stacy laughed in pure joy. She hadn't realized how boy-hungry, how fun-hungry she was. All these weeks of striving to be the unusual girl for an unusual job which called for tact and strength of character. All these weeks of putting up with Mrs. McKibben's cold-shouldering, and with Eve's shifting moods, and having only Fabian with whom she felt completely at ease. These past weeks had been a strain on a girl who loved people and was upset if she wasn't loved in return.

So today she beamed at old and young, and old and young beamed at her. Nobody stood on ceremony. Boys and girls came up to be introduced, and the not so tall but much more talkative one would say, "Miss G. R., meaning gorgeous redhead, this is Reverend Doolittle, the famous evangelist and saver of souls. And this girl he's with is Peggy, one of the fallen he picked out of the gutter." If an unattached boy came up, Stacy would be pulled closer between the two and introduced as Miss Hands-off. "She belongs to us, so don't anybody ask her to go to the Grange dance tonight because we're about to and she's about to accept with pleasure."

Another boy would be introduced as Alf the Ax, and Wild Bill, who was not at all wild, would murmur to Stacy, "Don't mention his prison pallor —he's sensitive about it. He's just done time for chopping up his grandmother."

It was pure corn, but Stacy loved it. She loved being with these two laughable, likable comedians. In the background was the singsong chant of the auctioneer, mixed with the frantic squeal of a pig or the timid baa of a sheep. From the barbecue pits came wisps of smoke and smells of delectable food.

She looked about for Mr. McKibben, and sought him out where he was talking in a group of men. "Will you let me know when they start selling the calves?" she asked him.

"Sure, sure, I'll let you know. It'll come later, after they serve dinner—yes, later. You go on and have a good time with your sidekicks."

"They said something about my going to a dance with them at the Grange Hall tonight. What do you think?"

"You want to go?"

"Oh, yes."

"You're on your own, girlie, to say aye or nay. I never heard anything bad about those boys. They're hard workers at the garage for all their damfoolishness."

A man in a red-checked shirt mounted an up-ended barrel. His face was the same hue as his shirt, from tending a quarter of beef over red-hot coals. He beat on a bread pan with a heavy spoon to get attention, and cupping his hands to his mouth, bellowed out the old cowboy call to dinner, "Come and get it, folks, before we throw it away."

Stacy's "sidekicks" went through the line with her. Thick slices of barbecued beef, potatoes, and baked beans were piled on the tin plates they held, and dippersful of gravy ladled over all. Pickles, rolls, and butter were already on the tables, and at the end of each, women were cutting homemade pies and dishing them onto thick saucers.

The stoutish woman at Stacy's table asked her if Mrs. McKibben had found a horsehair sofa yet. Stacy shook her head without further comment. She would like just one day free of museum details.

But the dispenser of pie continued, "I met you that first day you stopped at the museum with Fabian. Remember my showing you the one pillow sham? Do you know that I simply can't find out what happened to the twin to it? So I decided I'd just have to make up another one—"

Oh, no. Not more about embroidered pillow shams.

Stacy sidetracked her with "Did you bake this cherry pie? I never tasted one so deluscious."

No one noticed or corrected her garbled word, and her ruse succeeded. "Yes, I made six early this morning. Maybe you'd like another piece?"

Stacy would.

The shorter of her two escorts asked her, "Do you always eat this much?"

"Whenever I can get it," she admitted.

"And groceries going up by the hour. Remind me not to propose. About this invitation to the Grange tonight which you are about to accept with pleasure—" A waiting pause.

"You're on your own," Mr. McKibben had told her. Imagine not having Ben to lay down the law to her! Yet she didn't feel the joyous relief she expected. She felt sobered instead. She even heard the echo of Ben's "You can't go out alone with a boy on the first date. You have to know him better."

"Can we take Eve with us and make it a foursome?" she asked. "She's at the McKibbens' too. You know her, don't you? Mrs. McKibben's niece."

The pause was very slight. "Sure, we know Eve. We get a little fed up with hearing about all the boys who worship at her feet. Okay, tell her to wash behind the ears and come along."

"Is it a dress-up dance? Heels?"

"Yes, ma'am. Wear shoes. It's the midsummer Grange dance, and everybody wears the best she's got—he's got."

The men and Mr. McKibben were gravitating

toward a low corral from which came a continuous bawling. "They must be starting on the heifers, and I want to be with Mr. McKibben," she told them.

"Get along to your Herefords, Miss Goody Two-shoes, and we'll poke around and hope we can find us an anvil. Do you know the 'Anvil Chorus'?"

"From Verdi's *Il Trovatore*. Sure."

They looked at each other, and the shorter and more articulate said, "Think of that. Our pearl is a cultured pearl. We didn't even know it was *from* anything."

"What do you want an anvil for?"

"Didn't you know? We're to be the village blacksmiths on Centennial Day. We work on outfitting a blacksmith shop after work. That's why we didn't burn up the road to the McKibben ranch to see you. Well, that's part of the reason. And that's what we're growing the foliage on our chins for. We're hunting for old horseshoes, too, but not for luck."

The nontalker put in, "We're looking for leather, too—a big hunk of it."

"For leather aprons," Enrico, the talker, explained. "Besides muscles, the village smithy had a leather apron. We've got a swell idea for Centennial Day—"

"Please," begged Stacy, "please spare me on early-day Starbrush and the Centennial. I get it at the McKibbens' from morning till night. Did you notice how fast I gulped down my second piece of pie? I wanted to get away before that woman got back to her pillow shams."

The auctioning began in the cattle corral, and she left them to go hurrying toward it. The men leaning on the barred gate told her Mr. McKibben was inside, and they opened it just wide enough for her to squeeze through. She pushed her way over to where he stood, close to the auctioneer and the white-faced animal his helper held.

Her ears took a while to sift out the words the auctioneer chanted while his eyes turned swiftly and his finger pointed to first one man and then another, "—ninety, I'm bid—not enough, farmers —this gent says a hundred—and here's a hundred, ten from the blue shirt there—We're not selling setting hens, friends, but cow-mamas in the making—one, twenty—no, twenty-five from the corner—Why not a hundred fifty instead of wasting your time and mine—?"

Four times she heard his ringing "Sold!" with his finger pointing to Mr. McKibben. Four times she saw her boss nod and lift his hand in acknowledgment.

Stacy tugged at his arm. "That's your four now, Mr. McKibben. We'd better go."

He edged away from her, the better to see the red bodies and white heads of the ones huddled in a far corner of the corral, awaiting their turn. "There's one pretty and snug-built heifer there—nice markings, too," he muttered. "I'm just curious to hear the bidding on her."

Stacy took a tighter hold on his arm. "You've got your four. That's all you can get in the trailer, and all you can afford, you said. You'd better come on—because there's something about hearing everyone bidding that just sucks a person in."

He looked down at her resolute face. "You're a bossy little wench, girlie. All right, all right. We'll need some help loading up our four."

She liked the "we" and "our."

The help in loading the heifers in the trailer was supplied by Wild Bill and Enrico. It turned out, however, that they did the loading, and Stacy and Mr. McKibben supplied the help.

He was now all impatience to leave. "We'd better get going. The sooner we get these critters settled down in new quarters the better." No doubt, he was also thinking of getting home before his wife.

The boys pulled Stacy aside. They were both panting, for it had been a tussle getting the fourth frightened and stubborn heifer up the ramp. "Just one thing, sugar bun. Are you a bottle babe? You know what I mean. Some girls think going to a dance means dancing one dance and then sitting out in the car and tipping the bottle for four or five."

Stacy knew the kind of girl he meant, and she shook her head vigorously. She, too, was out of breath; she had helped hold back the three heifers already in the trailer while the boys maneuvered the last troublesome one in. "No, I like to dance too well. I'd rather dance than—"

"Eat?"

"No, drink."

"Fine. In case Eve gets ideas, it'll be three to one. It's not the principle of the thing; it's the money," the spokesman for the two assured her earnestly. "We have to hoard ours for anvils and leather aprons."

"We've already got the old forge and bellows," said Wild Bill. "Do you know what a bellows is?"

"No, and I don't want to know" were Stacy's last words as she turned toward the station wagon.

They reached home at milking time. A swift glance assured them that the panel truck, in which Fabian and Mrs. McKibben had set forth that morning, was still absent. Stacy, following orders, pulled up close to the calf pen. Vrest came from the cow barn and set down his half-full bucket of milk. Stacy helped the men unload the huddled heifers and coerce them through the wide gate of the pen. She helped them back the trailer into the shed.

Vrest's approval of the purchases added to Mr. McKibben's boyish elation. He slapped Vrest on the back and said, "You and I might as well start growing whiskers like all the other jackasses for the Centennial. Otherwise folks might take us for tenderfeet."

Yes, one needed to take Eve's moods and attitudes with that spoonful of salt. When Stacy told her about the dance and the planned foursome, she pooh-

poohed not only "those two goofballs that think they're Jack Bennys" but Grange dances.

"They're just one holy mess. Women and smelly babies, and old grandpas, and gawky kids that want to dance with you."

But when Stacy started dressing in her junior escort turquoise and tying back her hair with a silver ribbon, Eve got herself into a V-necked yellow sheer with a wide set-in belt of cotton lace.

Stacy entered the Grange Hall smiling. She danced to the hillbilly music and hummed under her breath. She held small babies while their mothers danced. Eve picked and chose her partners, but Stacy danced with scuffling-footed young boys who approached her with such shyness that she helped them along by asking, "Want to dance this with me?"

And when a very old gentleman regretted to her that he couldn't dance the new dances because in his day he had danced polkas and schottisches, she said, "I can polka and schottische." (Her Irish uncle was right, too, when he said that dancing came as natural to an O'Byrne as trotting to a horse.)

"Would you dance a schottische with me if I get the musicians to play one?"

"I'd dearly love to."

Stacy and the old gentleman danced what was a one-couple exhibition of hopping, gliding, and whirling to catchy two-four time. Stacy was extrovert enough to love it, and also the clapping and hurrahing when the music stopped. And when her partner bowed to her, she made him an old-time curtsy. He was very short of breath, but he managed a gallant "Thank you, my dear. Even in the old days, I never had a partner as pretty or as light on her feet."

"The sweetheart of Starbrush," Eve called her.

"It's been a glorious, gladsome evening," she told the boys as a good-night.

The next morning when Eve turned over in bed and muttered thickly, "I just can't get up," Stacy went down the stairs singing. Her day at the auction, her night of dancing, all the nonsense she had talked, and the compliments she had heard were like a shot in the arm. She felt light-headed, exhilarated, and in love with life again.

Even Mrs. McKibben's aloof response to her good-morning didn't silence her singing. She broke off to say to Mr. McKibben and Vrest, "I'm glad I'm not a hermit."

Vrest gave his throat-constricted laugh. "When you are a hermit, we will see white blackbirds."

11

While Stacy helped Eve with the supper-getting the next evening and while they waited again for Mrs. McKibben and Fabian to return from Starbrush, they reminisced about the people and happenings at the dance the night before. They had to raise their voices above the wind and the clattering of the washbasin on the stand outside and the complaining murmur from the brass dinner bell on its wooden arm.

Queenie whined at the door, and Stacy let her in. Her thick fur was fluffed out in all directions by the wind that swooshed through the kitchen, scattering a pile of green paper napkins and lifting Mrs. McKibben's appliquéd apron off its hook. They had no sooner gathered them up than Mr. McKibben came in on another gust, which banged the door after him and again scattered green napkins like leaves and left the apron in a huddle on the floor.

He was muttering to himself, and he muttered on to Stacy about the homesick Dormeir heifers he had let out to graze and how they had spent the day hunting for, and finding, weak spots in the barbed-wire fence. He glowered with a certain uneasiness at Eve as he muttered.

He went to the wall telephone and carried on a shouted conversation, as he always did. Under cover of it Eve confided to Stacy, "He thinks maybe I'll tell Aunt Evvy about his buying more Herefords. But I won't. Not unless," she amended, "I get good and mad at him."

Mr. McKibben hung up the phone and turned to Stacy. "Tell you what you do, girlie, you drive up to Les Payne's place. It's not far. Les and his boy aren't home, but his wife says they'll be there any minute. Most likely by the time you get there. He's owed me fence posts for a year. He'll load them in the car for you. That way Vrest can get at the fence the first thing in the morning. This wind will die down with the day."

He took out his usual stub of pencil, and finding a piece of paper, drew a rough sketch of the road and the two turns she must take.

The back of the station wagon could be, and usually was, made flat for hauling. It was so set this windy evening when Stacy got into it. Eve ran out for a final word. "The posthole digger, too, Uncle Mac said. They borrowed it when they got the posts. Those Paynes are good at borrowing, but not so good at bringing back."

Stacy had no trouble finding the Les Payne ranch. The woman who walked out to the car to meet her and said, No, the menfolks hadn't come back yet, was the same one who had talked pillow shams to Stacy on her first day in Starbrush, and the one she had diverted from the subject yesterday by praising her pie.

But there was no escaping pillow shams this windy evening. Mrs. Payne seated her in the kitchen with a glass of fresh-churned buttermilk and promptly brought out *two* to show her. "Now this is the *old* one you saw before." Stacy remembered the faded embroidery on it that traced out "I Slept and Dreamed That Life Was Beauty." It seemed to her that the woman might have left well enough alone. But, no, here was its twin when it came to hand-worked forget-me-nots and doves, except that it looked newer and read, "I Woke and Found That Life Was Duty."

Stacy could say to Fabian, "I'm sick to death of Centennial talk"; or to the boys she had dated last night, "Please, please don't tell me any more about blacksmith shops. You've already told me more than I want to know." But here in the Payne kitchen, she could only sit and endure.

She heard about the big problem, which had not been copying the embroidery, but trying to whiten the old and yellowed made-up square and to *un*whiten the new. "I'd boil and bleach the one and hang it in the sun. And then I'd dip the new one in coffee—and that would turn it a little too brown—"

Just to rest her ears from pillow shams, Stacy

broke in with "So many of my girl friends in Denver live in those new one-story houses they call ranch houses. I wonder why they call them that, because they aren't anything like the ranch houses I've been in out here."

It worked. Mrs. Payne said scoffingly, "Yes, I've seen pictures of what they call ranch houses. Land sakes, most of the houses on ranches out here were just two- or three-room shacks to begin with, and then were added on to—a room here and a porch there. Hardly any of them had bathrooms until about twenty—maybe twenty-five—years ago. That one of ours was the one I set my incubators in. The McKibbens made over their storeroom."

It was dusk when the dog's barking announced the return of the Payne menfolks. The wind was blowing harder when the rancher and his teen-age son loaded in the fence posts. It was dark by the time the lumbering fourteen-year-old, after hunting through tool shed, barns, and feed lot, found the posthole digger and made room for it in the station wagon.

The man, holding tight to his hat, said, "Heard on the car radio that they've had some good-sized twisters in Kansas today. We must be getting the tail end of them." He tilted his head up to the dark sky. "Mean-looking wind clouds. Maybe you better come in the house and see if it won't blow over after a bit."

But Stacy had had enough and more of Mrs. Payne and pillow shams. She muttered that Mr. Mc-

Kibben was waiting for her and opened the car door.

Mr. Payne told his son, "You ride down to the fence with her and open the gate, and show her our tracks going catercorner across the hay section. We always take that shortcut to the McKibbens'."

Stacy followed the car tracks the boy pointed out. At first they were clear in her bright headlights. She drove on, straining her eyes to see them through the wind that was stronger and was whipping up a dusty murkiness of grass and dust that snick-snicked against the car.

And then she lost the tracks. She wove this way and that, looking for them. The car lurched and dipped over the humps and hollows, with the fence posts rolling first to one side of the car and then to the other. And what an earth-shaking clatter that posthole digger made! She decided to back-track and go out the gate the Payne boy had opened for her. Better to get back on solid road. Better a few extra miles than meandering around in a hay meadow.

But she couldn't find the gate she had come through. She couldn't even find the fence. Her lights suddenly picked up a haystack, blurred of outline because of the wind's riffling and scattering bits of it. It was hemmed in by a barbed-wire fence.

She stopped the car. She sat there, her heart thudding in helpless confusion. It all had a night-mare quality—this being lost with no sense of direction, and wandering on and on, and finding no landmark. The flaying wind was like enemy hands, shoving at and almost lifting the car. But the car was her friend, dependable and staunch. She was safe as long as she was in the car.

Outside was a swirling blizzard—not a white one, but a dirty hay- and grass-colored one that hid the earth. Her eyes followed a wisp of hay that seemed to dance and swirl in the lights of the car. Like a mad miniature witch, it bobbed up and down, dipped and pirouetted, and then—almost with a bow—collapsed on the hood of the car.

The air was suddenly full of hay witches and misshapen hay birds—one was something like a skull. Stacy said in a laughing voice to build up her shaky courage, "I'm getting out of here right now before that haystack moves over on top of me."

She pressed down on the gas pedal and whirled the wheel for the turn. She had made half of her turn when the car tilted as though it had struck some lumpy object, and she heard the rasping grind of that something against the car's innards. Simultaneously the lights went out; the motor died; and the fence posts and the digger rolled over to the low side with a rattle and hard thump. The car tilted far over as the weight shifted.

In sudden terror that the car was tipping over with her in it on the downward side, Stacy opened the door and leaped out.

She didn't land on her feet but on her hands

and knees. Still in unreasoning fear, she scrambled on all fours to put a safe distance between her and that inimical thing of metal, which had once been her friend. She dropped down, fighting for breath.

Her hair was tugged and whipped in all directions. She held it protectingly over her eyes and face, and peered through it at the dark blob of car. It was an unmoving blob. Then the car wasn't going to tip over. It had just seemed so to her.

But she still felt safer here, crouching on the ground, even though the wind yanked her blouse out of the wraparound skirt and pelted her bare skin with its prickly, stinging load.

Over the roar of the wind she heard a crackle and snap behind her. She hugged the ground tighter and turned her head. It was one of the posts around the haystack that the wind had snapped off where it went into the ground. The wires were still attached to it, but the wind whipped it high in the murky air, held it there playfully though it quivered like a live thing, and then slapped it back toward the ground. *Yes, and the wind would have been just as impervious if it had been a live thing it tossed up and down in the air.*

She looked up at the sky. It seemed so wrong for the stars to be shining there, bright and serene, and quite unconcerned about whatever went on below.

That was the bone-chilling thing—the uncaringness of the elements. To the brutal wind Stacy

Belford was nothing more than the fence post it had snapped in two. She was at the mercy of a faceless enemy, incapable of mercy.

She huddled closer to the ground, her body bent over her knees, with the wind beating at and raging about her. It seemed aeons before she sensed that its fury was slackening. She could tuck her skirt in over her sore flesh, and it would stay tucked in. The tail end of the Kansas twister had either moved on or spent itself.

She still hunched there, bruised and beaten. Her knees and the palms of her hands were raw from her frantic crawling away from the car. Her eyes were sore, and sand gritted between her teeth. She scolded herself, "You can't sit here like a scared rabbit all night. Get going."

But she was too shaken and cowed. The night was chill, and she was shivering, but she only hugged her bare, chafed arms and sat on.

Another aeon passed before she saw two lights in the distance coming her way. Car lights. You'd think a girl who saw a rescuer heading toward her through a dark, unknown field would jump to her feet and shout for joy. Instead she only sat, shivering harder and clenching her jaw tight to keep back her tears.

Before she could identify the car as a panel truck, she saw the sign in the right-hand corner of the windshield,

COME TO THE
STARBRUSH CENTENNIAL
AUGUST 23

and that started her laughing. At least, she meant it for laughter.

The truck stopped close to the tilted station wagon. Fabian climbed out, and turned the beam of his flashlight on its empty seat. He flashed his light this way and that, calling to her. Her throat was so dry she was afraid he wouldn't hear her "I'm here." He came toward her. So beautiful—so beautiful, his white shirt and owlish face behind his glasses!

She stood up on cramped, shaky legs that promptly folded under her. He caught her and steadied her against himself. "Are you all right, young'un—are you all right?"

She couldn't answer for laughing and sobbing and gasping out that it was so—so funny—when she didn't want any part of the Centennial—and to look up—and see a sign about coming to it—Tears burned in her sore eyes, and ran down her grimy cheeks.

"But you're all right?" he kept asking, and tightening his hold. She could only nod and choke out, "I'm all right—I was—just scared—"

"That wind was enough to scare the wits out of anyone. Looks like you and the haystack got tangled up together." His chuckle wasn't as casual as he intended it to be. "Stop shivering. Wait." He got a flannel shirt out of the truck, and put it on her as though she were a wooden and helpless child. "Here, put your arm in here—no, the other arm." He flicked dusty grass out of her hair, and wiped the grubby tears off her face.

She answered his questions about the car—the rasping grind and the lights and motor going out. Fabian said it sounded like a broken connection.

She did what he told her to, as though her wits had indeed been scared out of her. He had her hunker down and train the flashlight's beam under the car so he could work on it. He found the broken piece of rake she had run over, and pulled it out. He discovered where the cable had snapped loose and mended it. When the lights were on and the motor running, he helped her back into the car.

"You all right now? You able to drive?" he asked with concern.

"Is it awfully late, Fabian? Was Mr. McKibben worried about me?"

"No, he went to sleep in the chair waiting for you. It isn't as late as you think. We tried to phone the Paynes, but the wind evidently wrecked the phone wires. Everyone just figured you were staying on there till the wind died down."

But when Fabian had started for home, he told her, he had decided to drive by the Paynes' to see if she had waited there through the windstorm. "They told me they wanted you to, but you said you were in a hurry."

Another time she would have made a glib remark about being in a hurry to get away from pillow shams. But now she pulled the flannel shirt closer about her and shuddered. She said in a thin and reedy voice, "I heard a crack and looked behind me, and there was that broken fence post. I could see the wind lifting it as high as it could when it was still fastened to the wires. The wind didn't know or care about me, not any more than a haystack—or the fence post—"

"I know, I know," he comforted. "I remember when I first felt that way about a blizzard—that it would just as soon freeze *me* stiff as a board as it would a sack of potatoes. I'll go ahead, and you drive along behind me. Okay?"

"And the stars kept right on shining up in the sky, Fabian. I always thought stars were friendly. Okay, I'll follow you. But don't go fast, will you?"

12

No trace of last night's violent wind riffled the trees that next afternoon when Stacy sat in the station wagon she had drawn up outside the museum block. She had parked there because it was the shadiest spot in the sun-drenched town.

Mr. McKibben had sent her to Starbrush to get some of the medicated oil he used for de-flying the cattle. "Doc Bledsoe knows what I use," he had told her.

Stacy had made many trips to the veterinarian, who also bred and trained horses on his acreage at the edge of town. His wife, a big-boned, easygoing woman, went to the stables in search of him for Stacy. He, in contrast, was a small, opinionated man who grumbled explosively over being called in from his riding ring. He would have to mix the prescription for her, he said. "So you're going to have to kill time for an hour and then come back for it."

Stacy sat in the McKibben car and watched the activity in the museum block with uninterested eyes.

A carpenter was working on the front steps of the Enos Starbrush house. On one side of it sat the first Starbrush school and on the other the first church. Both resembled a child's drawing of a house, with a pointed roof, one door at the end, and two windows on each side. The church was distinguished by its small steeple, which held a bell.

Never in her life had Stacy felt so depressed, so unsociable. If she had been her old self, she would have killed part of the hour by dropping by the Lindstrom garage. Not only did she feel incapable of lighthearted patter with Enrico and Wild Bill, but she had the shaky feeling that if anyone spoke to her, she would cry. She was hot and thirsty, but she didn't go to the drugstore for a Coke for the same reason.

She saw Fabian turn off Main Street and come toward her parked car. His arms were loaded, and he looked rumpled and hurried. "I've got something for you," he greeted her. "I was going to take it to the ranch, but when I saw you parked here—"

Even as she had feared, the tears came. He busied himself with his packages until she wiped her nose and eyes and said thickly, "This is the worst day I've ever put in. I can still taste dust and hay. I'm—I'm still shivery inside. You can't imagine—"

His smile and the nod of his head were full of understanding. "Yes, I can imagine. Did you sleep all right last night?"

She could only shake her head. So had last night

been the worst night she had ever put in. Although the wind had died down, she had closed the window tight, hoping to shut out her jitters. Sleep wasn't sleep but nightmares. Several times Eve had called out, "Stacy, wake up and stop screaming."

Fabian's sympathetic eyes rested on her wan face, but his voice was quite casual. "How about my getting you a Coke? Remember Arnold who came out to dinner the day Eve burned the rolls black? He keeps a few in the schoolhouse for us when we work on Centennial business."

"No, never mind. What've you got for me?"

"Hold this box of hardware a minute. Remember last night your talking about the wind not caring any more about you than about a fence post? It's what writers call the impersonal, implacable fury of the elements."

He sorted out a small book from the armful of odds and ends he carried. She noticed what nice hands he had—long-fingered, deft—and how he wet his finger and almost lovingly rubbed at a spot on the faded red cover of the book. "That's the thing I remember so clearly about this story. A young woman and her baby are alone in a dugout with a blizzard raging outside. I remember her going out and feeling that she didn't count against the vast, unbroken whiteness of the snow and the bitter, bitter cold."

He laid the book in her lap. "I hunted it up for you after I got home last night."

He didn't say as Katie Rose did, "You just

ought to read this." Or as the nun who taught lit at St. Jude's, "I'll give you three weeks to read the book and turn in your report."

He only said, "I hunted it up for you after I got home last night," and gave her his nice, not wide but understanding smile before he went hurrying off.

The title of the book was *Let the Hurricane Roar*; and the author, Rose Wilder Lane. And it was such a thinnish book. She opened it, and her eyes read the simple lines of the first paragraph:

> While they were children playing together, they said they would be married as soon as they were old enough, and when they were old enough, they were married.

She was still reading it and living with the young husband and wife as they crossed the plains and made a dugout into a home. She looked up startled when the driver of a rattly car honked at her and called out, "Hey, miss, the vet said to tell you it was ready."

She had no chance to read further in the book until supper was over. Mrs. McKibben was again on the topic of the Songbird of Starbrush, and of adopting a song the Songbird had written on Colorado as the theme song for Centennial Day. Fabian, looking most dubious, kept repeating, "We'll want something lively and catchy."

Eve broke in with, "Oh, for Pete's sake, Aunt Evvy, everything that poor Milly wrote is so mopey. What is there lively or catchy about 'Oh, Colorado, We Sing in Thy Praise'?"

Mrs. McKibben said doggedly, "The whole idea of this Centennial is to perpetuate the memory of the Enos Starbrush family."

It was a relief for Stacy to take her slim book and go upstairs. There was no bed lamp to read by. Only an unshaded globe dangled in the center of the ceiling and was pulled on and off by a cord.

She propped herself up on her cot. She read of the young couple fixing up the dugout and moving into it. She had to read on to see how the girl came through the birth of the baby. Ah, nice, the husband making it a cradle out of packing boxes and smoothing down the wood with a broken piece of lamp chimney. She sat up straighter in bed, and with an ache in her chest, read of the black cloud of grasshoppers descending and devouring their beautiful wheat—and dreams. The suspenseful what-will-they-do-now held her. . . .

She was scarcely conscious of Eve's coming to bed, of her transistor radio whispering out love songs, or even of Eve's "Are you going to read all night?"

"Do you mind if I leave the light on a little longer?"

"The light won't bother me," Eve said.

"The husband has to go back east to get a job," Stacy murmured in explanation. She just couldn't close the book and leave the wife and baby alone in the dugout miles from everyone. The blizzard struck. The woman wadded up wild hay and fed it into the stove to keep her and the baby warm. The husband returned in the last few pages.

Stacy closed the book on the couple's happy reunion and her own satisfied sigh. She got up and pulled out the light, and turned off the radio the sleeping Eve had left on.

Lying there on her cot in the dark, listening to the chirping crickets and the bawling cattle, it took Stacy a while to come back to the summer of today, instead of living in a dread winter almost a hundred years ago. And to come back to herself after being inside another young woman's skin. So this was what "losing yourself" in a book meant.

She had never realized before how by opening a book you could be transported from one geographic location to another, or from one century to another. Or that printed pages could lift you out of your depressed self. It comforted her to know that another young woman in different, yet similar, circumstances had also been cowed by the uncaring, unmerciful elements. Yet that woman had accepted it as part of life, and Stacy breathed to herself, "The next time, I'll know what to expect."

Fabian came for breakfast the next morning. His early arrival had to do with taking Mrs. McKibben to Starbrush before the painter started his work. Stacy was setting the table when she heard the labored chug of the panel truck.

She hurried out to meet him, still clutching a handful of silver. She had been humming "Rose of

Tralee," and she sang out to its tune, "I couldn't put that book down—I just had to see—whether it ended as happy as could be."

His eyes lighted. He sang back without breaking the melody, "Now you are a reader—and I am so glad. For now your bad days—won't be half so bad." He took her arm as they walked to the house. "This God's-in-his-heaven mood fits you—better than that all-is-lost one you were in yesterday."

She was still under the spell of the book and the harrowing hardships of the characters as she sat at the table and poured syrup on her pancakes. She burst out, "I never realized before how awful hard it was for those early settlers. Just think, not even water. They had to dip it out of a creek. Not even matches. They had to rub stones together. I never thought before how lonely and scary it must have been for Enos Starbrush to see the wagon train moving off and leaving him and his family out there alone on the prairie."

Mrs. McKibben actually gave her an approving smile. Stacy added, "I don't blame you, Mrs. McKibben, for wanting to *perpetrate* his memory."

Dead silence fell. Mrs. McKibben's face lost its smile. Every eye, intent and puzzled, turned on Stacy. Oh, dear, she had met that puzzlement before when she garbled a word. She groped frantically in her mind for the four-syllable word, beginning with *per*, she had heard Mrs. McKibben often use in speaking of the Starbrushes and the Centennial.

Stacy corrected herself quickly, "I'm sorry, I mean *perforate* his memory."

Eve gave a shrieking giggle. "Try *prevaricate* his memory," she said.

"Try letting him lay," Mr. McKibben grunted, and got up from the table.

Wouldn't you know. Whatever I say or do, or don't say or do, just makes things worse between Frozen-face and me.

Fabian said in his nice schoolteacher voice, "I find a lot of people have trouble with that word, *perpetuate*."

Fabian brought Stacy another book that afternoon. Mr. McKibben and Vrest were baling the cut alfalfa and having trouble with the baling machine. Stacy had driven Mr. McKibben back and forth between the field and the tool shop while he hunted up tools and hardware in an effort to repair it.

But there was no repairing the broken part. It would have to be taken in to Lindstrom's garage for a welding job. Stacy was at the edge of the field waiting for Vrest to disjoint the part, when Fabian drove down to give her the book. He handed it to her with the same remark, "I hunted this up for you. I think you'll like it. Have you seen the movie of *Gone With the Wind*?"

"No, they were just starting a rerun of it when I left Denver."

"Good, the book will be new to you then."

It was a paperback but a very thick one. She weighed it in her hand and said in dismay, "But this one's so heavy—and so thick. Haven't you got another little, thin one? Oh, my heavens, Fabian. *Eight hundred and sixty-two* pages. There's something about a big, chunky book that scares me off."

He was climbing back into the panel truck. "Well, read the first chapter—or the first few pages—and see if you like it," he said, and waved her good-bye.

While she waited for the men to bring the piece of machinery she was to take to Starbrush, she opened the book. . . . And was introduced to Scarlett O'Hara, with her green eyes and magnolia-white skin, on the porch of Tara talking to the Tarleton twins. . . .

The book rode on the seat beside her while she drove into Starbrush. Lindstrom, at the garage, apologized for how long it would take them to do a good job of welding. He added, "The boys went up to the blacksmith shop while things were quiet around here." He meant that if she found waiting tedious, she could go up there.

She didn't. She sat in the car and turned to where she had left off in the book. For now she was all anxiety about Scarlett—poor Scarlett, who had just received the crushing news that the boy she loved was going to marry another.

She had finished the first chapter and was in the second one when a deep, sepulchral voice said,

"This is your friendly undertaker. I dig you, honey babe."

It was the shorter and more talkative of the two who were designated as lady-killers, quiz kids, goofballs, and lover boys. "Did you know that tomorrow is our glorious Fourth of July?" he asked.

"Yes, but I hear Starbrush isn't going to celebrate it in their usual style because they want to save all their steam for the Centennial."

"Righto, my little Tinker Bell, but how about your going with us blacksmiths to a celebration at Elmore? A rodeo in the afternoon, and then we'll buy you the chicken supper the Ladies' Aid puts on at the church hall. They always have beets, and nothing makes stewed chicken look gorier than beet juice on it. And then if it doesn't rain, there'll be dancing on a platform outdoors.

"Sounds wonderful. I don't think Eve is going any place," she suggested.

"Okay, we'll take her, too, and even it up. Only I had you the last time, so Bill will get you and I'll draw Eve this go-around. I know no gentleman mutters a mutter about a girl, but does she have to keep telling about her poet friend that calls her a wood nymph?"

Stacy's laugh spilled over. "The way I heard it, an artist friend said she had the eyelids of a faun." She added guiltily, "But Eve's okay."

"I'm sure she means well," he said with a sly grin, "but you're the one that warms the cockles of my heart."

"I'm always glad to be a cockle warmer."

"I'll start working on my parents to get the car. We could ride you in the jeep, but not two females."

"I'm reading *Gone With the Wind.* Have you ever read it?"

"Nope. The only thing I read are the comics in the paper. Especially 'Peanuts.' "

She wished he had read it. She wanted to say to him—or to someone, "I could just hear those crazy Tarleton boys wondering why Scarlett didn't ask them to stay to supper."

When she returned to the ranch with the mended part of the baler, and before she told Eve about their invitation to the Fourth of July celebration, she asked, "Have you ever read *Gone With The Wind,* Eve?"

"No, but just as soon as I go home, I'm going to see the movie."

"Scarlett is so real. I was glancing ahead to where she's deciding which dress to wear to a party. Doesn't this sound pretty? 'The green plaid taffeta, frothing with flounces and each flounce edged in green velvet ribbon, was most becoming, in fact her favorite dress, for it darkened her eyes to emerald.' "

Eve said generously, "It'd be pretty on you."

Stacy told her then of the invitation to the rodeo, church supper, and dance at Elmore. "I asked Mr. McKibben if he'd need me to chauffeur tomorrow, and he said no."

Eve said the dance sounded like fun. She added, "It won't make us very popular with Aunt Evvy, you know, to be getting so buddy-buddy with her sworn enemies."

"Her sworn enemies? Those two? How could they be anybody's sworn enemies?"

"If you'd ever listen to her museum and Centennial talk, you'd know how bitterly she resents their crowding in with their blacksmith shop. She fought tooth and nail to keep them out."

"Why? The Enos Starbrush house isn't the only one to be part of the early days. They're going to have the first church and the first school, too."

"Ah, yes, but the Starbrushes had their hand in starting the church and the school—but not the blacksmith shop. She's against anything that takes away from the Starbrushes. If you ask me, I think she's afraid the blacksmith shop might get more attention, and it just might, if those goofballs have a fire in their forge and maybe a horse to nail a shoe on. Aunt Evvy thinks they're brazen upstarts. Didn't you notice how cool she was to us after we went to the dance with them?"

"She's always at the freezing point with me," Stacy said ruefully.

"I just wish she'd be so mad at me for going with them tomorrow that she'd send me home."

"You're just exaggerating, Eve."

Eve gave her foot-high shrug. "Okay, so I'm exaggerating."

13

Wild Bill and Enrico came to the McKibben ranch the next day shortly after the noonday dinner. They were not in their jeep but in what was evidently the family car. Stacy went out to tell them that Eve wasn't ready yet.

Perhaps Eve's talk of Mrs. McKibben's enmity toward them was not wholly exaggeration, for when she added, "So come on in," Wild Bill said on a gulp, "No. No, we'll wait out here." She remembered then that neither had they left the car when they came to take her and Eve to the Grange dance.

Enrico said, "Go get your sunbonnet and wait with us."

"Why won't you come in?" Stacy asked. When there was no answer, she pursued, "Is it true that you and Mrs. McKibben don't like each other?"

"A truer word was never spoke," the shorter of the pair said.

The awkward silence that followed was broken by the shy, quiet one, "Do you know what? The fellow that had the first blacksmith shop came just a few weeks after Enos Starbrush did, and he was the one that fixed the wagon wheel Enos broke, and he was a great-great-uncle of ours, so haven't we got as much right to reproduce his blacksmith shop as she has Enos's house?" And then as though he were afraid of having said too much on a touchy subject, he added, "We think we've found us some leather for aprons. We know a fellow that's got a grandmother-in-law that's got one of those old fringed-leather riding skirts—"

His running mate took it from there. "But this friend of ours has to talk her out of it or else do her out of it. But she's had it wrapped up in newspaper and put away on a shelf in a closet for over fifty years, and she wouldn't ever miss it, this fellow says."

Eve joined them then, and Enrico said, "You get to sit up in front with me, Eve. Now is the time to tell you girls the sad news. What are parents coming to these days? Mine insist on having the car to go to the fireworks show the firemen always put on in Starbrush the night of the Fourth. So can you two bear up if we don't take in the church supper and dance? We'll have to make tracks for home soon as the rodeo is over."

Eve turned in the seat to demand of the tall boy in back with Stacy, "Why didn't you get *your* folks's car?"

He looked at her over the top of his dropped-down glasses. "My older brother beat me to it," he admitted.

"The only reason I'm going to this thing is to go to the dance," Eve said ungraciously. "I loathe and despise rodeos."

The two boys sat, looking somewhat wilted. Stacy thought for a moment that Enrico was going to say, "Then don't go, Eve, if you feel that way." But no one said a word until Eve herself finally flung out, "Well, if we're going, let's go."

The rodeo at Elmore was held at the fairgrounds. The unroofed grandstand was hot and very noisy, what with yelling children leaping from seat to seat and enthusiastic viewers cheering the rodeo participants. Everybody knew everybody else. Everybody knew the contestants, too, judging by the loud admonitions when a roper missed a calf, "Back to the bean field, Jocko," or the encouragement when one managed to stay on a bucking Brahman steer, "Be a hero, kid, and the girls will love you."

Enrico nodded toward the second bronc rider to come out of the chute. "He's from Starbrush. Still owes the garage for his snow tires, so cheer for him. If he wins some dough, maybe we'll get our money."

Eve grumbled about the hot sun and the noisy children. She drank Cokes and showed little interest in who stayed on his mount and who tumbled to the ground. But she showed bright-eyed interest in two boys who had moved about as close to her and Stacy as it was possible to get to girls who were with dates.

Wild Bill and Enrico saw a white-haired man named Donovan standing down in front of the grandstand. Donovan, they had heard, possessed an anvil, and they wondered if he'd be willing to part with it. It was Eve who said, "Well, go on down and ask him."

And Eve who lost no time in their absence in talking hurriedly to the two other boys while Stacy watched the bulldogging of steers.

The boys moved back a discreet distance, and Eve clutched Stacy's arm in joyful conspiracy. "We've got it made. I fixed up dates for us for the dance tonight. The black-eyed boy's name is Vern—Isn't he a honey?—he's mine. And his friend—see the blond with the sideburns—is for you. He's just drooling over you. He says he's got a thing about redheads."

"Eve, that's bird-dogging." Stacy could suddenly hear her brother Ben admonishing her and Katie Rose, *Bird-dogging is about as low as you can get. I'll skin you alive if I ever hear of you doing it.*

"Bird-dogging, my eye. Those two dodoes asked us to go to a rodeo *and* dance. They're the ones that are letting *us* down."

"They couldn't help it. Their folks had to have the car."

"Do you want to go to the dance and make a big night of it, or go home and twiddle your thumbs?"

She wanted to go to the dance. And Ben wasn't

here to skin her alive, and yet—and yet she found herself saying, "Eve, I wouldn't feel right ditching Wild Bill and Enrico. And you'll sure cook your goose with them if you do."

"Oh, I don't know," Eve said airily. "I'm no slouch at handling things like this."

She was certainly no slouch at telling a tall tale, Stacy realized, when Wild Bill and Enrico returned. She told them about meeting this old friend of hers, Vern. Why, she had known his whole family for years and years, and Vern was telling her how his mother was sick in bed, and just the other day she had been asking about Eve and wishing she could see her. "So I just feel I ought to go and—maybe cheer her up because—"

Enrico interrupted, "Did you talk Stacy into staying for the dance? Or are you walking out on her too?"

"Oh, now, who said anything about walking out on anybody?" Eve's tone was aggrieved, even reproachful. "It's just that the poor old lady was always so sweet to me and—"

"She knit you your first pair of red mittens, I'm sure," Enrico said.

Stacy looked up to meet the eyes of her gangling, shy, and whiskered escort. She noticed that the eyes looking over the dropped-down glasses were gray and straightforward. "Would you rather stay for the dance instead of going home with us?" he asked bluntly.

She couldn't honestly say she'd rather go

home with them, so she worded it, "I always go home with the guy that brought me."

As the stand emptied, she dropped behind to ask Eve, "What am I going to tell your aunt? What will she think about your staying on for the dance by yourself?"

"I'm not worried about what she thinks. I've got to have some recreation. I'm nobody's slave girl."

On the ride home, Stacy sat in the front seat between the driver and Wild Bill, all of them munching hot dogs. It was a quiet ride. The boys' blithe spirits were at a low ebb. Stacy wasn't sure whether it was because of Eve's giving them the go-by or because Donovan, the man who owned an anvil, had refused to part with it. His wife had a fern sitting on it, he told them.

"Maybe we weren't tactful enough," Enrico worried; and Wild Bill added morosely, "We got to have us another anvil."

Stacy even pretended an interest in anvils to cheer them.

At the McKibben ranch, the car was stopped close to the big cottonwood to let her out. "And from you, Miss Bright-eyes," Enrico said, "let's hear no more of 'How about taking Eve?' We can make room in the jeep for the three of us. So you'll have to make room in your heart for both of us. Right?"

"Right," she said, and waved them good-bye.

The ranch seemed deserted this early evening.

Only the dun-colored Volkswagen huddled under the long shed. No panel truck; she had hoped Fabian would be there. No pickup either; come to think of it, she had heard Mr. McKibben and Vrest mention the safe and sane fireworks display in Starbrush. Not even Queenie was at hand to waddle out to greet her.

But as she reached the door, she saw Queenie coming from the chicken coops. Behind her was Mrs. McKibben with a basket on her arm. She was gathering the eggs. She stopped in front of the granary. This building was raised about two feet off the ground so that the floor and the grain stored on it would not absorb dampness. The space under it had not been closed in but was left open for housing the wheelbarrow and shovel used for transferring the feed to the sheds.

Stacy had helped Eve gather eggs, and she knew that a few of the hens preferred laying eggs under the granary rather than in nests in the henhouse. She walked toward Mrs. McKibben and said, "We get a few eggs there every evening."

"Yes, I know." The woman stood irresolute. Her bulky, unyielding body could never manage to crawl in after them, Stacy realized. And she, ever eager to please in spite of her protests that she didn't care whether Mrs. McKibben hated her or not, said, "I'll crawl under and get them. Eve and I have a system."

One had to crawl so close to the ground that it was impossible to back out carrying the eggs. The system was for the crawler-in to lay the four or five eggs on the shovel, back out, and then carefully pull the shovel out after her.

Mrs. McKibben actually smiled at this feat. The smile made Stacy so happy she didn't mention that she had snagged one of her best stockings in the egg-getting process.

They walked to the house together. Stacy held open the door for Mrs. McKibben and the egg basket. Only then did Eve's aunt realize her niece wasn't home. "Where's Eve? Didn't she come home with you?"

"No, we had to leave early—the boys did. But Eve met some old friends, and she wanted to stay on a while and visit with them." If Eve's aunt doubted that old-friend bit, she was too proud to question Stacy further.

"Have you had supper?" she asked.

"We had hot dogs and pop. I'm not very hungry. I'll just have a glass of milk."

She opened the refrigerator to get it. There sat three quarters of a cake with thick chocolate icing, and Stacy gave a spontaneous gurgle, "Um-mm, you baked a cake."

"It's my chocolate torte."

The woman cut her a generous wedge. Stacy ate it and drank her milk while Mrs. McKibben sorted and put the eggs away. "It's deluscious cake," Stacy praised. Again she saw the puzzled look in the eyes turned toward her, and she stammered, "I guess—I mean that's not the word I want. I'm always getting them mixed up—but the cake is heavenly."

Mrs. McKibben unbent further. "A cook always likes to hear a compliment even if the word isn't in the dictionary. Men wolf down whatever is put before them without ever a word of praise."

She's actually unthawing toward me. Please heaven, don't let me say anything to make her freeze up again. Stacy thought of asking if the menfolks had gone to the fireworks display in Starbrush, but decided against it. And she didn't dare mention the rodeo to which she had gone with the woman's sworn enemies. She said, "I'm reading *Gone With the Wind.* That Scarlett is quite a hussy. I can't wait to see if she can persuade the fellow she's in love with to elope with her. Have you ever read it?"

"No, I haven't. I ought to read more, but I never seem to find the time. I'm going to be telephoning the women on my committee this evening, so if you want to read—"

This was dismissal, and Stacy recognized it. "I'll read upstairs," she said promptly.

She walked very softly up the steps. This newborn friendliness was so delicate, one must tread carefully.

The evening breeze had not yet cooled off the bedroom under the sloping roof. Stacy sat on the cot and took off her shoes and stockings. Well, this certainly wasn't a very glorious end to a not very glorious Fourth—this missing a dance and then being shunted upstairs to a bedroom before it was even dark. She peered out the window at a wispy quarter of moon barely showing in the graying sky. What a lovely night to be dancing on an outdoor platform.

She sighed, and opened her book.

14

Stacy had never realized before what a perfect cure a book is for feeling lonely and sorry for one's self. Propped up in bed and utterly engrossed, she barely noticed when the ranch pickup returned late that evening with Mr. McKibben and Vrest. She read on and on. It was past midnight, her eyes were heavy, and she was looking for a place to stop when the light that hung from the ceiling flickered briefly and went out.

Again it took a full minute to move herself back from a plantation in Georgia to an unfinished guest room on the Colorado plains now in darkness because the bulb had burned out.

She was wondering if she should go downstairs and hunt for another bulb so that Eve would have a light to undress by when she heard her come home. Stacy slid quietly out of bed, and felt her way to the stairs and down them to the landing and the door opening into the big central room. It was ajar.

Before she could call softly to Eve to bring up a new bulb, she heard Mrs. McKibben speak from her bedroom doorway, "Is that you, Eve? I've been worried about you all evening."

"What was there to worry about?"

"I don't think you should have stayed on with someone else when you went with Stacy and—and those two. I didn't approve of your going with them, but as long as you did—"

Now here comes the old and dear friend routine, Stacy thought. But Eve said plaintively, "I'd never have gone with them if Stacy hadn't just wheedled me into it. Maybe it wasn't right to ditch them, but honestly, Aunt Ev, I just had all I could take of those two and their blab-blab-blab about their blacksmith shop and their leaping all over the grandstand, talking to people about anvils and things. Stacy thinks their idea of being blacksmiths on Centennial Day is oh, so marvelous, but like you say, what's a blacksmith shop got to do with Enos Starbrush?"

The wide yawn Stacy had started broke off midway. Eve's aunt, quite mollified, said, "We can hardly expect an outsider to have any feeling about our Starbrush Centennial."

Stacy turned back upstairs on that. The night breeze was chill now, and she was back in bed with the blankets drawn up to her chin when Eve came into the room.

"Are you awake, Stacy?" she whispered. "Do you mind if I turn on the light?"

Stacy too kept her voice down though it shook with fury, "The bulb's burned out. I went down to tell you to bring up a new one, and I heard you telling your aunt that I wheedled you into going to Elmore, and that I played up to the blacksmiths and their blacksmithing. And then I heard her call me an outsider."

Perhaps Eve thought she could handle this situation too, for she said airily but still in a near whisper, "Didn't you ever hear that listeners never hear good of themselves?"

"That's right. Not when they listen to a two-faced friend like you."

Unpredictable Eve. She didn't fight back. She said she didn't mind undressing in the dark. She started telling about the dance. Vern was simply wild about her. He was so jealous when she danced with his friend—"The one with sideburns that was simply ga-ga over you."

Flattery will get you no place. Stacy made no answer, and Eve went on, "Vern has to go to see his father—I forget where he said—but when he comes back, he and the blond want to make a date with us. He says—the one for you—that he'll wear his Kelly green shirt just to make a hit with you. Or are you still going to be loyal and true to the goof-balls?"

Another silence, and Eve asked, "Aren't you even going to talk to me?"

"Why should I talk to a snake in the grass?" Stacy's whisper was more of a hiss. "Anything I say, you'll twist out of shape to your aunt. You want her to hate me and treat me like an outsider."

"Everybody else likes you better than they do me," Eve defended. She began to cry. "It's all right for you to be so—high and mighty about—about lying. You've never had to—but I have to. Life would be just hell for me if I didn't."

She waited for Stacy to ask why. When she didn't, Eve went on as though she had, "I'll tell you why. My stepmother hates me—she always has—and she's always running to Dad and telling him I'm going to the dogs. She was the one that couldn't throw my things in a suitcase fast enough when Aunt Ev called and said Uncle Mac needed a driver."

Stacy pretended to be asleep. But she lay awake long after Eve slept. She had hoped the thaw would last. She had been so happy this evening during that brief time of friendly give-and-take—the near folksiness—that Stacy hungered for. And then to have Eve spoil it all.

In the hot July days that followed, Mrs. McKibben again gave Stacy the frosty treatment. And she, angry and hurt at the one she blamed for it, gave almost as frosty treatment to Eve.

Fabian was the only one she could open her heart to. She couldn't to her impatient and explosive boss, much as she liked him. She couldn't to the two in the Lindstrom garage. They phoned her often. "This is Mack the Knife. Where can I meet you to carve you up?" She saw them in Starbrush. "Aw, please, come up and see our bellows." But she couldn't explain to them how much it grieved her to live under the same roof with someone who disliked her.

"She liked me that night when I came back from Elmore, Fabian, and got her eggs out from under the granary—yes, and ruined my best stockings. She really did. She gave me a bigger chunk of cake than she needed to. Then that Eve! Telling her that I'm simply drooling over her sworn enemies!"

"Too bad Mrs. Mac can't take her with a grain of salt."

She was holding his glasses while he washed and dried his face and hands at the side of the house. How naked, defenseless, and not at all studious, his face looked without them.

"Grain of salt! A whole cupful you mean, don't you? Is it true about Eve's stepmother being such a monster?"

"Not that I know of. But Eve has a sort of *idée fixe* that all stepmothers have to be villains. I feel sorry for anyone who builds up fantasies the way Eve does."

"Don't you feel sorry for me?"

He gave her his rare and radiant smile, and shook her lightly. "Not you, beautiful bundle, as your admirers call you. Because all the fairies came to your christening, remember? Because you have songs popping out of your seams."

"I wish Mrs. McKibben didn't hate me."

"If I have to tell you once more that it isn't you, redheaded Stacy Belford, that she dislikes,

I'll shake you. She's an unhappy, humorless woman, and she—"

Again the conversation was broken off by Eve coming out and clanging the dinner bell.

Several days later on her way home from Starbrush, Stacy made feeding Fabian's ducks an excuse to stop and talk to him.

"Fabian, I still can't see why Mrs. McKibben is so bitter about the boys and their blacksmith shop. I got lured into looking at bellows, forges, and anvils, though I'm not sure which is which. And you know how I hate old-time doings, but I think it'll be fun the way they plan to swing the anvils and sing the 'Anvil Chorus.'"

"Lord's sake, Stacy. It'd take two men even to pick up an anvil. They're going to swing the hammers *on* the anvils while they sing. And did they tell you they're going to have a horse there and nail a shoe on him?"

"Oh, yes, they told me all. They've located an old white, paunchy, good-natured horse that they hope won't mind if they pound a nail where a nail isn't supposed to be pounded. Does Mrs. McKibben know that the first blacksmith here fixed the wheel Enos Starbrush broke when he crossed the river?"

"Indeed she does. And it doesn't seem to sit well with her. Do you remember wondering why the lover boys who wrote the note and stuck it onto the salt block didn't follow it up by coming out to call on you? I'll tell you why. Because the very next night, there was a Centennial meeting, and that's when Lindstrom brought up about reproducing the blacksmith shop. Mrs. Mac fought it. They both lost their tempers in a pitched verbal battle. She lost, and she's not what you'd call a good loser."

"Hurrah for Lindstrom!"

"He's a stubborn Swede. Do you know about the Capulets and Montagues?"

"Oh, sure. I played Juliet in our school play this year. It's just in pronouncing words that I'm stupid."

"You're always good for a laugh, young'un. Well, the feudin' Capulets and Montagues have nothing on the Lindstroms and Mrs. Mac. How are you doing with Scarlett O'Hara?"

"I'm halfway through the book. Right now, Scarlett is sick with worry for fear she'll lose Tara—you know, the old plantation home—for taxes. I can't wait to see if she can borrow the money for them."

The book, along with Fabian, was Stacy's lifesaver. Evenings were something to look forward to.

When her mother telephoned one late afternoon, Stacy barely gave her time to tell about the family before she broke in with, "Mom, have you ever read *Gone With the Wind*?"

"*Gone With the Wind*! Bless you, child, I read it before you were born. If I ever get time, I'd like to read it again."

"I never thought the Civil War was anything like that. I never thought about it, period. Scarlett is so selfish and bullheaded, but I can understand what made her like that and feel sorry for her. I can hardly wait to read more of it. Did you ever think I'd be the kind that couldn't put a book down?"

"Will miracles never cease! I read a piece in Sunday's paper about the Starbrush Centennial."

"Yes, Fabian wrote that and got it in the Denver paper."

"It said what date it was, but I've forgotten."

"August 23. And by a coinstance, that's the day—"

"*Coincidence*, honey."

"Well, that's the day Mr. McKibben's ninety-day time of no driving is up." Stacy added on a giggle, "He says Starbrush is celebrating it for him."

"And you'll be home right afterward?"

"Yes, the day after the big celebration. I'll drive Mr. McKibben in, and he'll get his license back so he can drive home himself. And Fabian—you remember the boy in the back seat with the antiques?—he'll come in with us, because he wants to buy a camper and get settled before the university opens."

"The write-up said Mrs. McKibben is a granddaughter of—"

"Great-granddaughter of Enos Starbrush. And she's dedicating her life to making the Starbrush house a dead ringer for the one old Enos lived in, including the horsehair sofa that she and Fabian drovc hundreds of miles to find. Including the organ that Milly, the Songbird of Starbrush, composed dreary songs on. Only Mrs. McKibben thinks Milly's a Miss Thomas Moore."

"Don't be flip and uncharitable, my own. The reason you feel sorry for and understand Scarlett in the book is because the writer showed you what went on inside her and what made her tick. Maybe if you could see inside Mrs. McKibben, you'd understand better what makes her tick and why she—"

"Mom, don't be lecturing me when you're on long distance."

Mother laughed. "That's right, or Ben will be lecturing me when the phone bill comes in. Just one more thing. That guitar player Pete is still stopping by to ask when you'll be back. I'll tell him August 24, and maybe he'll stop pestering."

Stacy thought fleetingly when the call was ended that she might have asked her mother if she had heard whether Bruce, her one-time boy friend, had come back to Denver. . . . No, Bruce belonged to the past, just as the guitar-playing Pete belonged to the future. Now was now, with Fabian for serious talk and the goofballs for lighthearted banter. . . .

15

Mrs. McKibben invited the Centennial committee to a buffet supper party at the ranch. Seventeen members, counting herself and Fabian, and *not* counting Mr. Lindstrom, her enemy.

"You know why she's putting on this big feed, don't you?" Eve asked Stacy with her know-it-all air.

Stacy and Eve were again on friendly terms. Neither of them were the kind who could harbor a grudge for long. "You don't have to have a *why* to put on a party," Stacy countered.

"Aunt Evvy does. She's softening up the committee with her cooking so she can shove Milly's god-awful 'Oh, Colorado, We Sing in Thy Praise,' down their throats for the Centennial theme song. It's Arnold who's been digging his heels in, because he'll have to train the school band to play it. You remember Arnold that came out that noon, and how Aunt Ev threw such a fit because I got the rolls too brown?"

Stacy, picturing the carbon balls that had bounced on the ground when Mrs. McKibben dumped them out of the pan, laughed. "Just a little too brown. How did she get out of inviting Mr. Lindstrom?"

"She solved that ticklish situation by picking the last Thursday in July when she knew he'd be out of town."

There was another ticklish situation closer to home. The brash Eve brought it out in the open the day before the supper while her aunt was polishing the silver.

"What about Uncle Mac and Vrest, Aunt Ev? Will they eat with you and your committee?"

"No, just the members. None of them are bringing husbands and wives." But she looked troubled, Stacy noticed.

"Are they going to eat in the kitchen with Stacy and me after your company's had their pick of everything? Remember how Uncle Mac hates to eat late and how he can't stand eating in the kitchen? He told me once it was because when he was a boy only hired help ate in the kitchen."

"I know." His wife looked more worried. "I thought of serving them earlier before—"

"How can you?" Eve pursued. "You've got your rolls and chicken and everything timed for later. Why don't I just tell Uncle Mac to get Vrest to drive the two of them in in the pickup and eat at Ethel's?"

"No, no, don't you say anything to him."

Stacy, listening, knew that Mrs. McKibben was quite aware that her husband wasn't fond of Eve and therefore ruled her out as a go-between. She sensed, too, that the woman wanted her, Stacy, to serve as one. An imp of perversity prompted her, *Don't you offer. Make the old stiffneck ask you. Make her say, "Please, Stacy—"* And then she saw that the hand that held the silver creamer was shaking, and she heard again Fabian's "She's an unhappy woman."

Stacy couldn't help speaking up, "I could ask Mr. McKibben which he'd rather do—eat here early or go in with Vrest to Ethel's Eat Shop."

Mrs. McKibben didn't meet her eyes. "I'd appreciate it if you would, Stacy."

She fell into step with her boss when he left the house after the noonday dinner. "Mrs. McKibben is having a supper party tomorrow. It's a meeting, too, for the Centennial committee, because she thought it'd be more informal than the ones the banker has at the bank—"

"I know all about it," he broke in impatiently. "I can even guess what ax she has to grind."

She giggled at that. "Yes, poor Milly. But she wondered if you and Vrest would like to have supper earlier, because you know how long it takes everybody to get together—"

"No, we're not eating earlier in the kitchen so's to be out of the way before the company comes. We've already made plans."

"To eat at Ethel's?"

"No, at Doc Bledsoe's. That's right—that's right. His wife is a chairman of something or other on the committee. He'll bring her out early and take us back with him. We'll have a Dutch lunch and play poker. He'll bring us home when he comes to get his wife. You can tell her that." He always referred to his wife in conversation as "her" or "she."

It was his closing remark that somehow saddened Stacy. "Tell her she needn't worry about me being underfoot when she's perpetrating—as you put it—the memory of the noble Starbrushes."

But Stacy didn't tell Mrs. McKibben that. She only told her about the arrangements with Doc Bledsoe.

So on this last Thursday in July, Mrs. McKibben's activities were devoted not to the past but to the present and the gourmet food she would present to the Centennial committee. No canned or frozen peas, but ones gathered fresh from the garden. Newly churned butter for her hot rolls. No store-bought ice cream but that home-made in a hand-turned freezer.

The Paynes had borrowed the freezer and, true to form, had not returned it. Eve was dispatched in her aunt's car to get it back.

Stacy had no errand-running or chauffeuring to do because the menfolks were making the cattle sheds tighter for the winter. Always pleased at the thought of a party and still hoping to win Mrs. McKibben's favor, she kept offering her help. I'll finish the churning while you gather the peas."

And when Mrs. McKibben came in from the garden and said gratefully, "Oh, you've worked the butter and got every bit of milk out of it," Stacy felt such a rush of happiness that she had to swallow twice before she could say, "I'll hull the peas while you fix the rolls."

Eve was an interminable time returning from the Paynes with the freezer. And when she did, she told of the old-fashioned basque dresses Mrs. Payne and her daughter-in-law were making to wear on Centennial Day. "What about us, Aunt Evvy?" she demanded. "I suppose you'll drag that old mauve or magenta costume of Milly's out of a trunk for yourself. But what about Stacy and me looking like belles of the sixties?"

"Yes, we must see about it. It's just that there's been so much else to think about," her aunt answered absently. She dipped a teaspoon into the creamy mixture to be frozen and tasted it. "Um-mm, it could stand a drop or two more of lemon."

The buffet supper party was a rousing success. Stacy, helping Eve pass rolls and fill coffee cups and refill plates, heard the lavish praise heaped upon the cook-hostess.

The two girls washed and dried the dishes in the kitchen. Fabian took time to come out and help them put the sherbet glasses away on a high shelf. A relaxed and amiable group of committee members gathered around the cleared table.

The banker, whom everyone called Tim and who, according to Eve, was the kingpin of the men's division just as Mrs. McKibben was of the women's, started the meeting with "If we can stay awake after that feed, let's get down to business."

The dishes done, Stacy edged through the big room to the stairs. She heard Mrs. McKibben talking about Milly's song as being happily appropriate for the Centennial celebration. "It seems more than fitting to have our theme song one that was written by the daughter of the man who founded the town."

Stacy was in bed reading when Eve came up much later. She said disappointedly, "I was in hopes there'd be a fight, because Arnold and Fabian wanted no part of Milly."

Stacy held her finger in her book to mark her place, and looked up. She had to let her mind leave Scarlett on a cold, rainy day in Atlanta and come back to the house where a committee meeting was breaking up downstairs. Voices outside were calling good-byes. Cars were starting up, and driving off.

"Wanted no part of Milly?" she repeated vacantly.

"No part of the Songbird of Starbrush or her lumpy little song, I said. But the motion passed. Poor Arnold is going to have to train his kids to tootle 'Oh, Colorado, We Sing in Thy Praise.' He spoke his piece, and so did Fabian, about wanting something with more tune and guts, but all the others sided with Aunt Ev. I guess they figured it'd be biting the hand that fed them not to, after making away with all her food."

"Did Doc Bledsoe bring Mr. McKibben and Vrest back when he came after his wife? I didn't hear anyone drive in, but then I've been reading."

"No, Doc didn't show. It didn't seem to bother his wife because he didn't, but then she's the kind that nothing bothers. She'd have to be—married to him. When the doings broke up, she said she'd ride home with Arnold and not wait for him, because when men got in a poker game with a few drinks, they forgot they even had wives." Eve yawned widely. "Well, what's your Scarlett up to now?"

"She's going to marry a poor drip just to get money to pay the taxes on Tara so it won't fall into the hands of the enemy. Tara's her plantation home with big white pillars that she loves so."

"Better than the man she's going to marry?" Eve yawned again.

"Oh, goodness, yes. The only man Scarlett loves is the one she can't get."

Stacy wakened at her usual time the next morning. She was out of bed and wriggling her bare feet into loafers before a certain *un*rightness struck her. There was no slam of door under her, no rattle of milk buckets as Mr. McKibben and Vrest met. She listened for it. She heard only someone walking back and forth, back and forth, in the big room under her.

She glanced out the window as she thrust arms into her slipover. Queenie was stirring about restlessly, looking toward the house and toward the road leading from town. Stacy knew now that she had heard no sound of a car bringing Mr. McKibben and Vrest home. Even if it hadn't really roused her from sleep, she would now on awakening have remembered hearing it.

She went slowly down the stairs. There was no breakfast smell of coffee or bacon frying.

Mrs. McKibben was up. Then she was the one Stacy had heard pacing the floor. She was at the open front door and, like Queenie, looking toward the road that led from Starbrush.

As she turned away, her appearance added to Stacy's feeling of unrightness. She wasn't combed and powdered, and wearing one of her button-down-the-front dresses and an apron over it with bright, appliquéd pockets. Her hair was disheveled, and a robe was pulled over her gown. It was buttoned crooked, and Stacy had never imagined Mrs. McKibben buttoning a garment anything but straight.

She turned her eyes toward Stacy on the stair landing. There was neither friendliness nor enmity in them, only a blank desolation. Stacy blurted out, "He didn't come home, did he? Is something the matter?"

For only a brief moment the woman allowed the misery—and wasn't there fear too?—to show in her eyes. And then she veiled them, and pulled a mantle of pride about her disheveled self. "He must have—have been detained by—something," she said stiffly.

It was a definite rebuff, but after glimpsing the bleak unhappiness in her eyes, Stacy was not entirely put off by it. She stood irresolute a moment before she offered, "Let me make you some coffee."

She started for the kitchen, but Mrs. McKibben said, "Just a minute, Stacy." She moved woodenly to the sideboard and busied herself in straightening its cover. Without lifting her eyes from it, she asked in what was intended as a casual voice, "When you told Mr. McKibben about—about my having the folks out to supper—would you mind telling me—I mean did he seem—?" She swallowed as though her throat were very dry. "What did he say, Stacy?"

She repeated verbatim as well as she could remember the conversation about the supper and committee meeting, and Mr. McKibben's breaking in to say that he knew all about it.

"But you told him I would fix supper for him earlier, didn't you? What did he say then?"

"He said he wasn't eating in the kitchen so's to be out of the way before your company came. That's when he said he and Vrest would have a Dutch lunch and poker game at Doc Bledsoe's, and about Doc picking them up and bringing them back."

A fraught pause. "Did Mr. McKibben say anything—anything else at all?"

Stacy hesitated. But again there was that note of desperate urgency in the woman's voice. "Well—he said to tell you that you needn't worry about him being underfoot when you were perpetrat—I mean, perpetuating—the memory of the noble Starbrushes."

Why were those words like a blow to her listener? A chair rasped as Mrs. McKibben pulled it out from the table and dropped onto it in a knee-giving way. Her breath came heavily through lips without color.

Stacy said, "What I imagine is that—just like Mrs. Bledsoe said herself—Doc wasn't up to bringing them home. You know how it is when men are playing poker. Why don't you just phone the Bledsoes'?"

The woman didn't answer. She sat rigid, straight, and unmoving as a statue. Only her hands moved. She was twisting one through the other like one does who comes in out of the cold.

"Would you like me to call and see what goes?" Stacy asked.

The mantle of pride slipped a little, revealing once more that bleak fear. "I—don't know—whether it would—do any good."

But Stacy phoned. Mrs. Bledsoe answered, her good-nature still unshaken. "Well, hello, Stacy. Quite a blowout here last night. Doc barely made it to the couch. Mr. McKibben? Sure, hang on, and I'll round him up. He's been racketing around—in and out—out and in." She laughed in untroubled amusement.

In a minute Stacy heard the familiar shouted

hello that scarcely needed a telephone to carry a mile. She said, "I thought maybe you'd like me to come in after you and Vrest, Mr. McKibben."

"That's a good idea, girlie—a good idea. You get here as soon as you can, because the cows are waiting to be milked."

There was no need for Stacy to repeat the conversation. Anyone in the room could have heard him. And anyone in the room could see that his wife had gone limp—was it with relief?—and that her lips were working in an effort to keep them straight, even though her head was bent low on her chest.

"I'm off," Stacy said.

It wasn't until two days later at noontime that Stacy had a chance for a private word with Fabian. It was during his washing-up time at the side of the house.

"Gosh, Fabian, I thought sure the ice jam was going to break that morning when I brought Mr. McKibben and Vrest home. Because she was worried frantic. I still don't know why. I should think she'd have figured out that Doc Bledsoe mightn't be in shape to drive them home."

"She thought he wasn't coming back," Fabian said gravely. "She phoned before daylight to see if anything had happened, and Bledsoe answered. He's a feisty little fellow. He doesn't like Mrs. Mac, and it makes him furious because she doesn't speak to Mr. Mac. Besides, the doc had probably had a few drinks too many, and so he took it upon himself—"

"What'd he say to her?"

"He told her that her man wasn't coming back. That he'd had enough and too much of her rubbing his nose in her Starbrushes."

"Good heavens! Did Mr. McKibben hear him tell her that?"

"No. The poker game had just broken up. The one who heard it and told me about it was that blabmouth who works in Ethel's Eat Shop. He was there in the game too."

So that explained Mrs. McKibben's walking the floor in dreadful fear. And her sagging with relief when she heard her husband bellowing to Stacy to come in and get him.

The two men had been most untalkative on the drive back. Mr. McKibben had dozed fitfully in the seat beside Stacy. His only comment was in explanation of his holding his hand in front of his mouth, the sure sign to Stacy that he had removed the "cussed contraption." "Ate a lot of peanuts and potato chips while we played cards last night. Ought've known better."

"She was standing in the door when we drove up," Stacy went on to Fabian. "I thought sure she'd come hurrying out and tell him—well, tell him something."

When Stacy with her two passengers had stopped under the cottonwood, the breakfast smells came out to meet them. Mrs. McKibben was standing at the screen door, holding it open as though she were ready to step out and meet her husband and say something like "I'm so glad to see you."

Would she have stepped forth and broken the ice jam if Stacy and Vrest hadn't been there to witness it? Or did Mr. McKibben himself rob her of the impulse? For even before the car came to a full stop, he was out of it and heading for the cow sheds with never a glance toward the house. He called over his shoulder to the slower-moving Vrest, "Go ahead and eat breakfast, and then bring down the buckets."

He answered Stacy's "Don't you want breakfast, Mr. McKibben?" with "Later on—later on. I'll come in and have you soft-cook me some eggs, girlie."

Stacy thought aloud, as she often did with Fabian. "The day of her committee supper I helped her, and she was so nice—"

Fabian broke in, "It still gravels me—the way she railroaded Milly's song through that night. I backed up Arnold, but he didn't have the guts to stand up to her the way Lindstrom did about his blacksmith shop. Why she's so obsessed with resurrecting Milly along with Enos, I wish I knew. Is she trying to prove something to Mr. Mac? I'm not psychologist enough to understand what's driving her."

Stacy wasn't concerned about Mrs. McKibben and her Centennial. But she was upset and baffled that she, Stacy, was out in the cold again. It was as though that early morning had never been —that chilly morning when a woman in a robe buttoned crooked hadn't been able to hide her desperate fear.

Was it because Mrs. McKibben, an aloof and proud woman, was ashamed that Stacy had witnessed her anguish? Had her pride suffered still another jolt when her husband gave not a glance toward his wife waiting in the doorway but went striding off toward his Herefords?

Like Fabian, Stacy was not psychologist enough to understand why Mrs. McKibben was more distant than ever to her husband's chauffeur.

16

A week after Mrs. McKibben's fateful supper party, Stacy sat hunkered down on the cement floor of the open porch. She was murmuring soothing sounds to Queenie while she extracted burrs out of the collie's long, matted hair.

Fabian and Mrs. McKibben had gone off about their Centennial business. Eve had driven in to Starbrush for groceries. The quiet of the afternoon was broken by Mr. McKibben's working on the stock trailer. He was pounding down any protruding nails and smoothing off all rough edges, for Prince Eric was to occupy it.

Vrest had gone out to the creek pasture after him. When they returned, the Prince would be loaded into the trailer, and Stacy and Mr. McKibben would take him to another ranch eighteen miles away. August was breeding time on the plains, so that cows should calve in April.

Queenie, pretending that she craved a drink, slipped away from Stacy. She noisily lapped up water from her pan in the shade of the cottonwood, and then lay down, looking back at Stacy and thumping her tail as though to say, "I still like you, but I can't take any more of your pulling out burrs."

Stacy's eyes rested idly on the chickens that had sought the shade. Some stood with their wings drooping and beaks open. Others hopefully scratched up the dry dirt and fluffed it through their feathers.

She was just wondering if she would have time to read a bit about Scarlett O'Hara before Mr. McKibben was ready for her, when she saw Eve coming through the McKibben gate and up to the house with her usual flourish. She got out of the car, her arms full of packages, and called to Stacy to carry in the two sacks of groceries.

Eve dumped her armful onto the dining table. "We'll put the groceries away later. Just look what I've got." She ripped open one of the packages and shook out lengths of bright scarlet print. "They used to call this calico, an old lady told me. And look what I'm going to trim it with." This time she spilled through her fingers yard upon yard of narrow white lace. "This is for my Centennial dress—for my riding in the stagecoach at the head of the parade, which is where everyone with Starbrush blood in his or her veins is going to ride."

"Pretty, pretty. And you'll look pretty in that bright red."

"I'll wear a red ribbon around my hair, and it'll cover the dividing line between the black roots and the fading Capri Copper. One of my boy friends is an entertainer, and he says he always thinks of me whenever he sings that song about scarlet ribbons in her hair."

Now she was quoting compliments from an entertainer boy friend along with the poet and the artist.

"And just cast your eyes on this." From another package, Eve was shaking out the folds of a sheer, cotton plaid material—green plaid on a cream background. "This is the closest I could get to your green plaid taffeta that Scarlett wore. Remember your reading it out loud and thinking it sounded super? Remember it said the green velvet ribbon that edged the flounces turned her eyes emerald green? Well, you'll have to settle for green *cotton* bias binding. But that should be just as good in turning your eyes green."

"You mean you bought that plaid material and all that bias binding for a dress for me?"

"Sure I did. You know that five bucks less a nickel and two pennies I got from you and never paid back because Aunt Evvy hasn't given me anything but a dollar or two now and then, because she's putting all her spare cash into perpetrating and prevaricating—"

"Wait. Let me say it, and show you that I can. Into per-pet'-u-ating Enos's memory."

Eve laughed with her. "I like perpetrating better."

"But, Eve, that goods and the bias binding

cost more than five dollars less a nickel and two cents. How did you pay for it?"

"Never mind how much it cost. Not very much because the storekeeper is selling the makings for Centennial dresses at cost. Starbrush patriotism. And I didn't pay for it—it's charged. Didn't I tell you you could get anything on tick except bus tickets?"

"I'm no good at sewing," Stacy confessed. "Sometimes I get carried away and start something, but Mom always has to take over and finish it."

"I'm good enough for both of us. I'll have you know I'm an A-plus sewing student. Only you needn't think I'm going to make French seams in your dress—not when I don't have a teacher standing over me."

"I wouldn't know a French seam from a German one. Can you make our dresses on that old treadle sewing machine?"

"I've sewed on it before. I know all its sulks and tantrums," Eve said confidently. "Here's the pattern. Fitted blouse—they called them basques way back when—and a long, tiered skirt. Your Scarlett O'Hara dress had a square neck, didn't it?"

Again happiness swelled through Stacy, and all but closed her throat. She had to nod her answer about the square neck. Unpredictable Eve. Maybe tomorrow she'd do some crummy thing, like pretending to her aunt that she had worked the butter when Stacy had, or laughing deridingly when Stacy called Enos Starbrush's *diary* a *dairy*. But right now Stacy loved her and was so happy that she threw her arms around her and said, "This is the first time I've even thought about *me* having any part in Centennial Day."

"We'll be devastating," Eve said. "I'll shake out the pieces of pattern and start cutting out right now while the table is clear."

Stacy stepped outside and looked in the direction of the creek pasture. Yes, there was Vrest in the distance, leading the arrogant, stolid, and slow-moving Prince Eric. She had to hurry back in the room to answer the telephone.

Her hello was answered by "Halo, Miss Ninny-hammer, halo. How would you like to ' 'ammer, 'ammer, 'ammer on the 'ard 'ighroad' with us blacksmiths if we swing by for you? We'd like you to rejoice with us. Remember Mr. Donovan that gave us a brush-off in Elmore about his anvil? His wife has been keeping a climbing fern on it, but she has a heart of gold and said we could have it and so—"

"The climbing fern?"

"No, you ninnyhammer, the anvil. We're going after it."

"I don't think a fern climbs. And I'd love to go with you, Enrico, but I have to ' 'ammer, 'ammer, 'ammer on the 'ard 'ighroad' with my boss and Prince Eric. He's being brought up from pasture now."

"Then will you promise to come and see the anvil at the blacksmith shop in Starbrush?"

"I wouldn't know an anvil if I met it in the road."

"We'll formally introduce you. Do you promise?"

"I promise." She hung up the phone.

Eve looked up from where she sat on the floor, surrounded by tissue-paper pattern. "Did they say anything about my going with them?"

"Not a word. What did you expect after your walking out on them in Elmore on the Fourth?"

"I had my own reasons for that."

"Not reasons. Reason. By name of Vern."

Eve gave a shrug and a mysterious roll of her eyes. "You can't always judge everything by what you see on the surface. I didn't want to tell you before, but when I was out here last summer, that crazy Wild Bill just lost his head over me. Believe me, I was actually scared he'd commit suicide. So I just thought—Okay, laugh."

"I always laugh at jokes like that," Stacy said, and gave an extra snort of glee each time she pictured the shy, gangling boy with his glasses down his nose, hopelessly impassioned over any girl.

Eve looked outraged, then sheepish, and finally joined in. "One of my boy friends is a writer, and he says that anyone with my imagination ought to write stories."

"He said a mouthful," Stacy agreed.

Mr. McKibben came to the door and called through the screen, "You there, girlie? Well, we're ready—we're ready—for you to back up the car so we can hook the trailer on."

"Be right with you."

August days turned hotter and drier. Eyes unconsciously lifted upward, hoping to see rain clouds forming in the deep blue of the sky. The murmur of the cottonwood leaves that Stacy had found so soothing now had a dry crackle. Ranch women lamented that their cabbages and melons wouldn't "make" if they didn't get rain.

Centennial Day was coming closer. Whiskers were longer, but tempers were shorter. Mr. McKibben's was both short and testy. Prince Eric was feeling the heat and his journeyings in the trailer over rough roads. His owner worried over him. Again and again Stacy drove him to Doc Bledsoe's for a tonic or change of feed for the prize bull.

Eve's enthusiastic fervor over her dressmaking had been replaced by fidgety grumbling over the bobbin's constant breaking of the thread. She had started out treadling the old Singer with her record player going beside her. By now the male voice that begged someone to take his hand and wander with him to Nowhere Land was worn and scratchy.

"Your grandmother's got an electric portable," Eve said to Fabian. "Why don't you bring it over for me to use?"

"Why don't I?" Fabian's smile too was a little more tucked-in these hot days. "Because Grandma has two great loves in her life. The car that takes her places and the sewing machine that makes her clothes for going places."

"For gosh sakes, Aunt Ev," Eve flung out. "Why don't you put this old antique in your museum and get a sewing machine that sews?"

"It's good enough for the little sewing I do" was the preoccupied answer.

Mrs. McKibben, seemingly oblivious to heat and drought, worked day in and day out at the Starbrush museum. "Everything from blacking the kitchen stove to refinishing Milly's organ," Fabian told Stacy with an exasperated smile that said again, "What is the woman trying to prove?"

When Centennial Day was only a week off, Stacy was on page 832 of *Gone With the Wind*. The book with its 862 pages went with her to Starbrush that morning when Mr. McKibben sent her to the bank with a legal paper. "Be sure you give it to Tim himself. To Tim, understand? Because those flunkeys working for him don't know their crazy bone from the rear end of a hack."

She had to telephone back to him from Starbrush to tell him that the banker had gone to Denver the day before but would be home on the afternoon bus. "Then wait for the bus," he shouted. "Wait there. You stop in at Ethel's and get yourself something to eat."

She didn't stop at Ethel's, because she was at a

suspenseful point in the book. She sought the shade of the block that was to be called Enos Park henceforth. But before she could find where she had left off in the book, she heard loud halloos from the blacksmith shop. The two were motioning to her to come over.

Ah, yes, the Donovan anvil she had promised to visit.

"This is it." Enrico pointed out the heavy iron stand with its flat top ending in a pointed snout. "So now we have two. This is the forge where we get the horseshoes red-hot. And here's the tub for water for dropping the shoes in to cool them."

"If you have the forge to get them red-hot, why do you have a tub of water to cool them?"

"Because, adorable dumbbell, you couldn't nail a red-hot shoe onto a horse's hoof."

Wild Bill interposed gently, "You have to get it hot so's to pound it into shape to fit the horse's hoof, and then—"

"Never mind, never mind," she stopped him. "You've already told me more about blacksmithing than I want to know."

But she had to back up and admire the sign over the door: BLOUNT'S BLACKSMITH SHOP. (Blount was the name of that first smithy, the forebear of the Lindstroms, and fixer of Enos's broken wheel.) She had to hear again about the paunchy and placid horse they would nail a shoe on during the Centennial Day celebration.

Enrico said, "Did you know I can sing as good

—well, almost—as the fellow who once bore my name? That's why I call myself Caruso. We'll give you a preview." To the rhythmic and resonant wham of the big hammers on the two anvils, the boys sang out a line of the "Anvil Chorus." Enrico's voice was loud and full, and Wild Bill's as wispy and uncertain as his growth of straw-colored beard.

The two had come to the blacksmith shop on their noon hour, and they left for Lindstrom's garage reluctantly. "You sure there isn't anything that needs fixing on Mac's old rumblebus there?"

"Not today," she told them.

Alone once more, she opened her book. The shifting sun gradually robbed her of shade. She didn't move the car. It was simpler to move herself to the back seat where the sun wouldn't be in her eyes.

Once, glancing up, she saw Mrs. Payne coming down the street. Mrs. Pillow-sham Payne on her way to the Enos Starbrush museum. These last pages were so much more engrossing than matching pillow shams which didn't quite match that Stacy huddled on the floor of the car, out of sight, until the woman passed.

The arrival of the bus and, with it, the banker reached through her absorption. She bent down the corner of page 849 to mark her place and drove to the bank. She caught the banker at the water cooler and gave him Mr. McKibben's paper. He would have detained her with talk of the Centennial parade

—"They tell me I'm to drive the covered wagon"—but she smiled and backed out as though she had pressing business.

Which she had. The book had built up to such an emotional climax that she *had* to read those last thirteen pages before she drove home. She sat in the car at the side of the bank without bothering to hunt any shade.

Without realizing that black clouds had blotted out the sun, she bent closer over the print. Because Rhett Butler, with bitter eyes and wintry smile, was telling Scarlett he was leaving her and just how she had killed his once great love for her. Stacy came to Scarlett's last words, "Tomorrow, I'll think of some way to get him back." . . .

Oh, but could she? The thought of Scarlett's losing him just when she realized that he was the only man she had ever really loved was more than Stacy could bear. She had to see Fabian. He was mending furniture in the workshop of his grandmother's house today. Stacy had to ask him, the fount of all wisdom, if he didn't think Scarlett had a chance to win Rhett back.

She drove swiftly down the one main street, turned at the filling station, and took the familiar road. The rumblings of thunder were now ominous growling roars. The sky was black—a purplish black—so that the yellow zigzags of lightning showed up with startling brightness.

17

She reached the turnoff of the road that led to the low Brown house, set among trees, with its screened front porch covered by woodbine. As she got out to open the gate, the first spatter of rain struck like a fusillade of bullets. She could see and smell the spurts of dust they raised on the dry earth.

She was struggling with that tight, barbed-wire gate and finding it harder than ever with her hands wet from the rain, when the raindrops suddenly changed to hail. They pelted her head, her bare arms, and her hands like sharp pebbles.

She gave a panicky glance at the car behind her, and another at the house ahead of her. She couldn't go on being pummeled while she tussled with the gate. She squeezed herself under its low wires, straightened up, and ran for the house through a curtain of hailstones. She tried to hold her purse over her head for protection. But it was too small to do much good. Besides, with her slipping and slithering in the hail on the ground, there was no holding it there.

She pounded frantically on the kitchen door. She tried the knob, and the door opened. Fabian was already hurrying toward it, and he stopped short. “Good heavens, Stacy!” And then, even as he had asked her the night of the windstorm, “Are you all right?”

“Oh yes—and this time I wasn’t scared.” But again she was half laughing, half crying, as she panted out, “Your gate’s so hard to open—I thought it’d be quicker—I mean I left the car outside the gate—but off the highway. Look at where a hailstone hit my arm—they must have put razor blades in some of them. Ooosh, and I’ve got them in my sandals.” She bent over to pull one off her bare foot. “Just look at how I’m dripping on your floor.”

“Hold still a minute.” He brushed embedded hail pellets out of her long, wet hair and off her shoulders. “I always seem to be brushing muck out of your hair. You shouldn’t have gone racing through the storm. Why didn’t you wait it out in the car?”

She laughed through chattering teeth. “I never thought of that. I was in Starbrush and I finished my book, and I couldn’t wait to ask if you thought Scarlett would ever get Rhett back. I know she was heartless and bullheaded, but she—”

“Never mind Scarlett now. Let’s get you dried out first.” He lit the oven of the gas stove and left the door of it open. “Wait a minute.”

He hurried out of the kitchen and came back

with a great armful of chenille robe. "Take off your wet things and get into this old robe of Grandma's. I'd better see if all the windows are closed." He said from the doorway, "Put your wet things on the oven door to dry."

Alone in the kitchen, she pulled her T-shirt off over her head and stepped out of her shorts. Her scanty underthings were not so wet but what they'd soon dry on her.

The robe had evidently once been rose-colored, but much wearing and washing had faded it to a lavender pink. Stacy's wet and goose-pimpled arms slid gratefully into the shapeless sleeves. She drew the ties snug about her waist—it would almost lap round her twice. It was long, and it dipped even longer at the seams.

"Are you decent?" Fabian called; and to her, "So decent you can hardly find me," he came in with a towel for her wet hair. They added her sopping green hair ribbon to the assortment on the oven door.

No hail pounded like galloping horses on the roof now, but a heavy rain sloshed past the windows. Stacy sat in the rocker Fabian had pulled close to the oven door. Her feet were curled under her for warmth, and the yardage of faded chenille enveloped her while she worked at drying her tumbled hair. She gave one last convulsive shiver, but it was more of cozy happiness than of chill.

She fumbled a comb out of her purse and ran it through her hair. Fabian said, "Your wet hair is the color of a copper kettle. Are you hungry?" And with his quirk of smile, "Foolish question. I should know by now you're always hungry."

"I'm hollow as a gourd. I was so busy reading I forgot to get something at Ethel's Eat Shop."

"Whatta you know! A chance to use up some of my duck eggs. Do you like them?"

She couldn't remember ever having tasted any, but she said fervently, "I love duck eggs."

But first he put a Band-Aid on her arm where a sharp hailstone had broken the skin. His hands were splotched with gilt paint. He told her he had been touching up old picture frames for the Enos Starbrush house.

"Oh, please, Fabian, no horsehair sofas, no old daggertypes today."

He chuckled. "Daggertype fits one prim old sister better than *daguerreotype*. Won't you even rejoice with me because I persuaded Marcia Mills of Special Events on your Denver TV to come down and cover Centennial Day? With her sound on film. I'm so proud of myself because I talked her into it. The only reason she consented, of course, was because we went to the U together. She says these centennial celebrations are a dime a dozen."

"I second the motion."

"No girl with a face as red as a baby's spanked bottom should act so hoity-toity." He was looking through the cupboard. "I've got stale crackers. I was thinking of feeding them to my Lauderbach clan.

But here's something one of the museum women gave me that I was saving for a special occasion. A jar of pickled peaches. Do you like them?"

"I just love pickled peaches." In her rhapsodic state if he had asked her if she liked ground glass, she'd have said, "I just love ground glass."

The scrambled duck eggs, stale crackers, and the sticky sweet peaches were a banquet to Stacy. Under the tenting of chenille, she pulled her knees up under her chin. Her toes curled in delight at being here with Fabian, snug and warm.

So much to talk about. And such a luxury, this talking without fear of being overheard, or interrupted by Eve's popping out a door to sound a loud and unmelodious bell.

"I can hardly wait to see Katie Rose and say, 'I just couldn't lay that book down.' " She added soberly, "Just think, I won't ever have to be lonely now that I can read."

"I don't imagine loneliness will be one of your problems."

They talked of the ending of *Gone With the Wind*, and whether Fabian thought Scarlett would win back her husband. He thought the author meant for each reader to decide the yes or no for himself.

"Scarlett was such a dope not to know until too late that he was the man for her," Stacy grieved. She broke a companionable silence while Fabian puttered about cupboards and sink. "I keep wondering why Mrs. McKibben was so torn apart that morning when she thought the mister was leaving her. I keep wondering why they stay together when neither one pays any attention to the other."

Fabian looked up from the skillet he was drying. "Because they love each other," he said.

"But if they did, they'd be reconcided, wouldn't they?"

He tipped his head in a considering, schoolteacherish way. "Recon*cided*? Now that's interesting. That seems to fit the meaning of the word better than recon*ciled*, because it gives the idea of being on the same side. Yes, I can see how it'd be hard for you to believe that those two mulish, hardheaded people love each other. Love has many sides, many facets. It isn't always hand-holding and billing and cooing."

"That time you were in love, were you awful hard in love?"

"Sure. As I said, I suffered all the pangs of unrequited love—even as poor Milly with her 'What of My Shattered Heart?' Have you been in love?"

"Oh, lots of times."

He laughed. "And you will be a lot more times." He stood on at the sink, and mused. "It's awful—I mean pathetic—the craving for love, for being noticed, for a little approval in every human heart. Especially the lonely ones."

Eve had said Fabian had been unloved and unwanted, she remembered. "Were you lonely, Fabian?"

A reminiscent look came into his eyes. "You

might know a kid was lonely who'd want ducks to keep him company. I was lonely for a mother." Another looking-back pause. "I always fell in love with motherly schoolteachers. I've noticed in my teaching experience that fatherless girls are more apt to fall in love with men teachers. It isn't love, of course, it's a schoolgirl crush, but it's the same heart-lifting, heart-crushing deal."

So much to talk about. They talked of Eve. "I like her," Stacy said. "Her bragging about all her boy friends and the near suicides doesn't bother me so much. There've been so many bothery things this summer. I don't know how I'd ever have gotten by if I hadn't had reading to take my mind off them. Or if I hadn't had you to turn to."

"I'm glad, young'un. Your heart is as warm as the color of your hair. I wanted to save you any hurt I could."

He gave her a smile of rare sweetness. She drew a sharp breath on something like a stitch in her side, only it was the exquisite but frightening thought, *I'm in love with Fabian.*

The realization stunned her. She had found out that very first day when they talked together at Pigeon Rock that he was comfortable to talk to. She had realized in the weeks just past that he was an old young man who saw more and understood more than most.

He was the first young person of the opposite sex who had ever given her credit for having a mind. None of the others had probed under her fun-loving surface. He was the first young man she had found herself longing to talk to, to ask questions of. And the first one she could unbutton her heart and soul to.

I'm in love with Fabian. It started that first day in Pigeon Rock, but I didn't know it.

She sat unmoving as though something very fragile and very precious was cupped in her heart and might break if she moved. She sat silent for very fear that if she opened her lips, she would cry out, "I'm in love with you, Fabian."

He still puttered about. She never knew when the rain ceased and when the room filled with a roseate glow. She only thought it was her own roseate state.

Fabian opened the door wide, and a breath of wet, deliciously fragrant air pushed in. "Come here, Stacy. You have to see this."

A rainbow, so perfectly formed, so delicate in pastel colors, arched over the drenched world. Stacy could have cried from the sheer beauty of it and of this moment when she stood in the doorway, her shoulders touching Fabian's. *Their* rainbow.

"I never could go for that pot of gold idea," he was saying. "Isn't a rainbow blessing enough? Like this one following the rain that will bring the pasture up, and swell the old Rattlesnake, and help make cabbages and melons—"

"And perk up Prince Eric. Because he was feeling the drouth and the heat."

"And if the Prince perks up, so will Mr. Mac's disposition."

Stacy laughed giddily. The laugh caught in her throat. "Fabian, when I'm with you—everything is so special. You're so—so special to me."

His eyes left the sky. He looked down at her glowing face. "I'm glad, young'un. Because you're pretty special—"

A noisy commotion interrupted. The flock of ducks were waddling across the wet grass still rimmed with hailstones. They were all quacking querulously, although Mrs. Lauderbach in the lead was the loudest.

"Looks like a protest march against the hail," Fabian commented. "I'll bet they're hungry. Should we give them some of our soggy crackers?"

The phone on the kitchen wall behind them rang a jangling two longs and a short. Fabian answered it. Stacy didn't need to ask who it was or what he was saying. It was Mr. McKibben wondering where his driver had been during the hail and the cloudburst. "She ran for cover here," Fabian told him. "She's on her way home now."

Oh, why did Mr. McKibben have to intrude into this ecstatic world of rainbows and Fabian? Why couldn't he have gone to sleep in his chair, as he had the night his driver was caught in the vicious wind?

The enchanted spell was broken. Fabian said, "I'll go up and bring the car down for you while you get out of Grandma's robe and into your clothes. They must be dry now."

She could hardly keep from clutching his arm and rebelling like a child, *I don't want to leave. I don't want to go back to McKibben's. I don't want to get out of this baggy old robe with the skirt dipping in scallops. I want to stay here and eat duck eggs and stale crackers and watch rainbows with you. It would be all the happiness I could ever ask for.*

But Fabian was already splashing down the wet road. He had reached the gate before she turned back to the oven door and her own dried-out garments.

He brought the car close to the house. "Go on now," he urged, "before Mr. Mac works himself into a tizzy. Never mind the gate. I'll close it when I go through."

She drove through it and onto the road. She looked back for a final glimpse of him, but he wasn't in sight. She felt again that near stitch in her side. *I'm in love with Fabian. I never thought I'd fall in love with someone so old.*

"You're pretty special—" he had told her. Yes, and if that Lauderbach clan hadn't interrupted and if the phone hadn't rung, he would have added, "—to me."

18

Stacy took her excited happiness to bed with her. And woke up, quivery with anticipation. When Fabian came at noon, it would take only a few words, or a conspiratorial smile, for him to say, "You're pretty special *to me*. I'd have said it yesterday if Mrs. Lauderbach and Mr. Mac had given me a chance."

She strained the milk the men brought in. In just the time it took her to fill three wide-mouthed jars, she was in three different places. First, in the house on Hubbell Street where she was saying, "Mom, this is Fabian. We're in love, and I don't care how long we have to wait till he gets his doctorate." Mother beamed and said, "I knew Fabian was an exceptional person that first day when I saw him in the back seat of the car."

Then Stacy was in the library at St. Jude's where her best friend Claire stopped her filing of books to say unbelievably, "No kiddin', Stacy? He isn't a football player, and he's twenty-*seven*?" And

Stacy was answering, "After knowing him, all the football players seem like overgrown infants."

Lastly she was in the doorway of the auditorium at St. Jude's, standing beside a corpulent figure in a black habit and saying, "Guess what, Sister Cabrina. This summer I read two books and fell in love."

Sister had no chance to answer because Eve came into the kitchen and announced, "I won't have enough green binding for one of the flounces on your dress."

Stacy's laugh bubbled over. "That's all right. What's one flounce, more or less, without bias binding?"

Fabian was late for dinner at noon. They were all at the table when there came that particular chug-chug of the panel truck. Then the splash of water from the outside faucet into the washbasin. But it would be so *obvious* if Stacy left her place at the table and went hurrying out.

Her heart beat with an uneven swush when she looked up to meet his eyes. He gave her no conspiratorial smile but only, along with everyone else at the table, a weary exasperated one.

He had driven to Elmore to pick up the five hundred Centennial Day programs. And found that the printer had spelled Starbrush, Star*bush.*

"He'll have to do them over," Mrs. McKibben said harshly.

"He's going to. But it'll mean another trip after them."

When dinner was finished, it was Mrs. McKibben who walked out to the truck with Fabian, not Stacy.

Each day the tempo of Centennial activities increased. Everybody made demands on Fabian. How many quarters of buffalo should the firemen order for the supper? Which should go first in the parade, the covered wagon or the stagecoach? Arnold was often with Fabian, fluttery and sputtery over his handful of boys and their struggle to make "Oh, Colorado" sound like something other than a doleful lament.

Fabian, working overtime, was seldom at the McKibben ranch these days. If only Stacy could find a few minutes alone with him.

But the plains had greened, and the cabbages flourished, and a cool, sweet breeze rustled through the cottonwood at night. Prince Eric's head lifted, and with it, Mr. McKibben's spirits.

Eve, too, stitched all those yards of lace on her ruffles with less grumbling. Not because of the weather, but because the black-eyed Vern was back in the Elmore country and was coming to Starbrush's Centennial. "He says he's counting the hours. He says red is his favorite color."

The blacksmiths phoned Stacy again and again. Wild Bill had to tell her, "We got our leather aprons. Remember the riding skirt we told you about?"

"The what?" she answered, her mind and heart wholly on when she could have a few private words with Fabian.

"The leather skirt for our aprons. The woman gave it to us. She's had it since she was sixteen, and she's seventy-one now, and we had to cut off the fringe. We want you to see the aprons, and see if you think we ought to drag them over the garage floor some more so they'll look—you know, old and sort of wornout."

Enrico, like the man he was named after, was giving more thought to the vocal number. He phoned to say, "We need your advice, sugar bun. Should I sing out—with Wild Bill's feeble help—the first line of 'the Anvil Chorus'? You know, 'Pour me a tankard—' and then sort of ta-*da*, ta-*da* the rest?"

"No, I'd say to sing two lines, and then ta-*da*, ta-*da*."

"Just as you say, Miss Cultured Pearl. What is the second line?"

She took a minute to hum through it. "I can't remember—exactly. Something about wine alone does something." And then her voice fairly sang out, "I tell you, I'll ask Fabian. He knows everything."

Here was an excuse for her to hunt up Fabian. She couldn't very well run him down as he busily handled details in Starbrush and say, "Now finish that sentence about my being very special *to you*." But surely she could demand a few minutes alone with him to settle a vital question pertaining to Centennial Day. Then, having disposed of Verdi's second line, she could say, "That afternoon of the hail and duck eggs and rainbow was the loveliest in my whole life." And he would turn his beautiful, understanding smile on her. . . .

Her chance came the next day when Mr. McKibben wrote a letter which he had put off writing for a week, and then decided it must be got in the mail posthaste.

The letter disposed of at the Starbrush post office, Stacy turned the station wagon to the block Mrs. McKibben was already calling Enos Park. It was an anthill of activity. Pits were being dug for the barbecuing. Outdoor tables were being built. She drove around the block twice before she located Fabian. He was talking to some workmen who were erecting a hot-dog and hamburger stand.

She sat for a moment, hoping he would see her. But she had to call to him to get his attention and motion him over. He walked toward the car with a "What do you want?" frown on his face. Oh, dear, this wasn't her envisioned romantic moment alone with him—not with this background of sawing and pounding, and some wafted snatches of music that must be Arnold's band at practice.

She said, flustered, "I told the boys I knew you'd remember what the second line was. They'll sing two of them—I mean the first two—because I don't see how they'll have wind to sing any more and swing the anvils—"

"Hammers *on* the anvils," he corrected automatically, looking at her blankly.

Dear heaven, the interruptions. A truck with

building supplies stopped beside the McKibben station wagon, and the driver called to Fabian, "All right for me to drive in to unload?"

Fabian nodded and turned back to give Stacy momentary attention. "I still don't know what you're talking about, young'un."

"The boys—the blacksmiths—asked me what the line was after 'Pour me a tankard,' and for the life of me I couldn't remember. It's something about wine alone does something."

He didn't say, "And you're bothering me about that!" but the exasperation in his voice did. "Who'll know what words they're singing? No one. The music teacher is having her girls' chorus sing Milly's 'Oh, Colorado' song, and no one will hear a word of 'the plains rolling gently—' and 'the mountain's blue haze.' And a good thing. So your lover boys could belt out 'Pour me a tankard' and then ''Tis wine alone that gives me St. Vitus's dance,' and not a soul would know the difference."

He left her to oversee the unloading of the lumber.

That night, long after Eve had ceased her chatter, Stacy lay wide-eyed in the darkness. Something was wrong. A man, no matter how bustling and burdened he was, could still squeeze out a minute for the girl he loved. But didn't all his actions, all his words add up to his loving her? There must be some reason for his not picking up where he had left off when the Lauderbach clan and Mr. McKibben interrupted.

She took out her memories of their times together, and sorted through them. Each shining moment of the hailstorm afternoon she relived. His fingers *had* been loving when he brushed the icy pellets out of her hair. He had said it was the color of a copper kettle, and that her heart was as warm as the color of it.

She moved back in time. The night of the wind Fabian hadn't gone to sleep in his chair. He had come in search of her. And then, understanding her awesome fear of the elements, he had put a book in her hand to read of others who had known that same fear. Or maybe he was already thinking that he wanted a wife who read books. *Ah, that stitch in her side again.*

She moved on back and back, to this meeting and that. To his saying all the fairies had been at her christening. Back to that first day in Pigeon Rock when he told her of his ducks, and his grandmother with an itchy foot and—

She sat up straight in bed on a gulp of breath. She had it—she had found the clue she was looking for. She had asked him, "Are you going steady with a girl you're going to marry?"

Here in the dark she could see again his rueful smile and headshake. "No, I'm not going steady. And no, young'un, I'm not thinking of getting married. . . . I wouldn't insult a girl by asking her to wait for me. I did once, and she gave me the merry ha-ha."

Of course, of course. It was all so simple. If

Eve hadn't been asleep, Stacy might have called out to her in this wondrous newfound happiness, "Poor Fabian is scared to tell me he loves me. Because once some greedy little gal didn't think he was worth waiting for, or being poor with. All I have to do is tell him I would—wait or be poor with him."

But these frenzied days, so packed full for him, were no time to tell Fabian. She would somehow get through the three more days till Centennial Day and the day itself. The very day after it she would drive back to Denver with Mr. McKibben and Fabian. There would be that lunch stop again at Pigeon Rock. Mr. McKibben would be sure to go to see his friend, Sweeney, at the Red Horse. And she and Fabian would leave the lunchroom to sit in the car until he returned. And this time, you could bet your sweet life, Stacy would let Mr. McKibben linger as long as he wanted in the Red Horse.

Her arms hugged her knees under her chin in shivery elation. The rustling of the cottonwood leaves, the bawling of the calves, and the soft cooing of pigeons provided background for her living in advance her time with Fabian at Pigeon Rock.

Mr. McKibben was one other person, besides Stacy, who was living for the day after Centennial Day when he would set out for Denver. "I want that license back," he told her. "I'm not kicking about you, girlie—not kicking a bit. You've been mighty good at sashaying all over the country for me. Just the same, I've felt like a hobbled horse. I'll be glad when all that damfool celebration is over. I want no part in it—no part at all."

"Same here," agreed Stacy.

But two days before Centennial Day, Fabian and Arnold drove to the McKibben ranch to tell Mrs. McKibben of the unexpected obstacle their parade plans had struck. An obstacle by name of Doc Bledsoe.

Doc Bledsoe, horse dealer and trainer as well as veterinarian, was providing the horses for the stagecoach; it was to be driven by the mayor and filled by the Starbrush descendants. He was also providing the four-horse team for the covered wagon. The committee had planned that the banker should drive it. But, hearing of it, Doc Bledsoe—to quote the fluttery Arnold—rose right up on his hind legs and pawed the air.

He had said, so Fabian told Mrs. McKibben with Stacy and Eve listening and Arnold putting in a cluck-cluck now and then, that there were only three men in the whole Starbrush country capable of driving a four-horse team to a covered wagon while a band tootled behind it. One was the mayor, but the mayor was already driving the stagecoach. One was Doc himself, but he was riding his palomino in the parade. The other was McKibben. So either Mac would drive the covered wagon or Doc Bledsoe wouldn't hitch his four horses to it, and that was final.

"Conceited little Hitler," Mrs. McKibben ground out.

"They're his horses," Fabian said wearily. "So someone will have to ask Mr. Mac if he'll do it."

Silence fell between the five. They all knew Mr. McKibben was not fond of either Fabian or Eve, mainly because his wife was. They all knew except Arnold himself that Mr. McKibben always referred to him as a prancy little pipsqueak. They all knew only too well that Mrs. McKibben was not in communication with her husband.

Fabian's eyes turned to Stacy, and she volunteered swiftly, "I'll ask him for you." She would have stuck her head in a lion's mouth if it would ease his tense worry.

"He'll do it if Stacy soft-soaps him," Eve said.

The two men drove back to Starbrush, and Stacy walked out to the home pasture where Mr. McKibben was oiling the windmill. She relayed to him the story of Doc Bledsoe's laying down the law about who he would allow to drive his four horses to the covered wagon and who he would not. "So that leaves you, Mr. McKibben."

"Did she put you up to asking me, now that they're in a bind for a driver?" Stacy, of course, knew who the *she* referred to. "Because, I didn't rate a place in the parade before—Oh, no, I certainly didn't rate driving the covered wagon old Enos was supposed to come in—oh, no!"

She could sense the hurt behind his belligerence, and she said, "Mrs. McKibben thought all along it was a mistake to have the banker driving the covered wagon, instead of you. Because it'll take a real horseman to handle them with the band playing right behind you." She murmured silently, "God forgive the lie."

The man stared off across the olive-green plains with an unreadable look on his weathered face. Stacy went on, "She's working herself to death—Mrs. McKibben is. So many of the women on her committee have let her down. Even the one that promised to find a bench and tubs and washboard to sit in back of the Starbrush museum said her arthritis—"

He grunted out, "She always took on too much." He pulled his gaze back to her. "Godamighty, I'm not supposed to look like old Enos, am I?"

"No, just like yourself," she said, and they laughed together.

"Then tell her I'll drive the covered wagon." His eyes narrowed with roguish malice. "And tell her that if I'd been driving it a hundred years ago, the wagon wheel wouldn't have smashed to smithereens crossing the creek—Yes, tell her that."

Stacy didn't tell her. Tact, Mother had said, was knowing when to open your mouth and when to keep it shut. She only reported to Mrs. McKibben that yes, her husband would drive the covered wagon in the parade that opened the Centennial Day celebration.

That same day Stacy found herself a participant in the Centennial celebration she had vowed she would have no part of. The teacher, who was coaching the girls' chorus in the singing of Milly's theme song, telephoned to her. Unlike Arnold she was not at all gushy and fluttery, but blunt and to the point.

"Fabian tells me you have a loud, strong voice, and I certainly need one to give a little body to these pipestems I'm working with. I told the chorus today that I had a two ninety-five music box that puts out more sound than all seventeen or eighteen of them. 'We sing in thy praise' indeed!"

"Fabian said that nobody cared what the words—I mean, that it was hard to hear the words."

"The words don't deserve to be heard. All I want is some noise to come from the truck load of us as we follow the band."

"I'll sing with your chorus," Stacy promised, without further urging. "I'll be glad to."

She was really saying, "I'd be glad to sing—or turn somersaults—just to make the day pass. Because the next day is my great, big, beautiful day."

19

On Centennial Day morning Stacy stood on Starbrush's back street in all the confusion of a parade getting under way. She was looking for the float with the girl choristers. She was also looking for her blacksmith friends.

She wore the green plaid dress Eve had made her. Its long full skirt was gathered onto the form-fitting basque. The bright green edging on two of the three tiers, and around the square neck, did intensify the green cast of her bright and questing eyes. But the right armhole of the dress was so tight Stacy couldn't lift her arm. She tried pushing up the long sleeve, but it didn't ease the restricting seam. This, in spite of all Eve's taking and jotting down measurements.

Stacy stood, lifting herself on tiptoe, clutching a handful of long skirt in one hand and a short, hooked, and evil-looking knife in the other. The knife, so the Payne boy told her yesterday, was what blacksmiths used to trim horn from a horse's hoof. He had unearthed it in their tool shop and entrusted it to Stacy to give to Enrico. "Tell him I sharpened it up good," he said.

She didn't see either Enrico or Wild Bill in all the noisy maelstrom.

The stagecoach was loading. There was Judge McKibben, looking even taller and more judicial in a black swallow-tail coat and high hat. There was Eve's father, looking boyish and embarrassed in the same attire. They had both come down last night and shared the bunkhouse with Vrest. Neither wife had accompanied her husband. The Judge's because of her hay fever and Eve's stepmother because—to quote Eve—she and Aunt Evvy didn't hit it off.

There was Eve in her bright red dress with its froth of white lace, looking like a red and white bouquet. Stacy felt again the pinching tightness of that one sleeve. *Eve, the A-plus sewing student. In a pig's eye!*

And there was Mrs. McKibben climbing into the coach. She was wearing what Eve called Milly's mauve magenta, and Milly, Stacy decided, had no more oomph in clothes than she had in songs. The dress was a dowdy poplin of muddy purple.

The covered wagon followed the stagecoach. Someone passing said to Stacy, "Isn't it wonderful? The governor came in time for the parade. He's riding in the covered wagon with Mr. Mac." Stacy strained higher on her toes to wave at him. But his whole attention was given to handling his four skittish horses.

Fabian was every place at once, looking as though he bore the weight of the world on his shoulders. He was wearing a red plaid shirt, and Stacy's heart could locate him easily, although there were a multitude of red plaid shirts bobbing about.

"Where will you ride in the parade, Fabian?" she had asked.

"I'll be on the ground, young'un. I promised Marce to stick close enough to brief her on who's who and why."

"Marce? I didn't know you knew Marcia Mills well enough to call her Marce."

"She went to school with me. Remember I told you?" And in a very conversational voice, "Once I lost a lot of sleep over Marce. She's the what-of-my-shattered-heart one I told you about."

Jealousy was suddenly a black and bitter taste in Stacy's mouth. "I don't know why you'd want her to come down to cover the Centennial. Why didn't you get somebody else?"

"How you talk! Because Marcia Mills's Special Event show is tops on TV, and she does a slick job on—"

"I don't like her. I think she was crummy to treat you the way she did. Who did she think she was anyway?"

He chuckled. "She knows who she was and is. A gal with goals and ambitions of her own, as you'll see when you meet her."

When they stopped at Pigeon Rock on the

way back to Denver, she would say to Fabian, "You're my goal and ambition."

The band passed by, ready to blare forth as it turned onto Main Street. And here came the float with the singers and their blunt-spoken teacher. Two girls reached down to help Stacy climb onto it. She felt the tight seam rip as she did. Over half her sleeve was pulled loose from its moorings.

The parade was on.

As it made its way along Main Street toward Enos Park, Stacy saw the camera set up and a man in a Hawaiian shirt turning its handle. She caught only a glimpse of Marcia Mills—a slim girl with bleached hair pulled back from a tanned face, which was partly hidden by dark glasses. She was talking into a microphone around her neck.

Again that bitter coppery taste. Was Fabian glossing over how he felt about her? Stacy had to see them together, so she could be sure there was nothing left of that shattered heart he was so casual about.

As it happened, when the parade was over Stacy literally stumbled into them both. Fabian and Marcia Mills had their heads bent over her reporter's pad when Stacy, stepping up on the curb, tripped on her long skirt, and pitched forward knocking both of them off balance.

"I'm sorry," she apologized breathlessly. "I'm not used to walking in long skirts, and I can't hold it up because I've got this hoof trimmer in one hand, and I have to hold my sleeve in with the other. I don't know what to do about this partly torn-out sleeve."

Marcia's clear gray eyes summed up Stacy and the sleeve situation. "Rip it all the way out, and the other one to match," she said. Fabian too gave it thought. "Yes, Stacy, it would look better than the way it is. And you can't go through the day holding a sleeve in place."

"But Eve made the dress for me, and I don't want to hurt her feelings."

Marcia said, "Whenever it's a case of hurting somebody's feelings or my own comfort, I take the comfort."

Stacy hadn't expected to like her. But it was hard not to like a girl in a mussed dress of wide navy and chartreuse stripes that was pulled lopsided by the weight of pencils, cigarettes, and pads of paper in its one pocket. Her sunburned nose was peeling, and she had evidently rubbed a greasy ointment on it. She wasn't Stacy's idea of a *femme fatale*.

The savory smell of frying hamburgers reached out from the stand. The cameraman, his tripod folded and camera hanging from his shoulder, was already munching one. Marcia unclipped the mike from around her neck and said, "Fabian, my dear love, I could do with a hamburger too."

"And coffee, I'll bet. Stacy, crowd in there, will you? There's Ethel behind the counter—Tell her who you want a hamburger for. I've got to see how soon they'll be ready at the church and school for you and the camera, Marce."

"The blacksmith shop too. We want to be sure and get that."

Fabian nodded without turning around.

Stacy's heart lifted like a bird on the wing. Fabian didn't love Marcia Mills. Stacy knew by the very way her "dear love" didn't register; by the very way he had turned her over to Stacy while he went about Centennial business.

"What do you want in your coffee?" Stacy sang out.

"Sugar and cream both. And all the trimmings on the hamburger. We've been up and on the road since four this morning."

The cameraman sat at the plank table with them. Marcia swiftly disposed of the hamburger and coffee as though food were sustenance and not something to dawdle over. "Don't you want that dangling sleeve ripped out? It's a mess, as it is. I'm a good ripper-outer. Let's see that hoof trimmer you're hanging onto." She tested it for sharpness, and then said in her capable and direct way, "You sit without moving a muscle, and I'll have you sleeveless in a jiff."

And so it happened that on Centennial Day, in a momentary quiet lull and with passersby stopping to stare, Fabian's old love ripped both sleeves out of his new love's dress.

Stacy thanked her and added, "Whew-w-w, that feels better."

She needn't have worried about Eve's feelings being hurt. She broke into Stacy's roundabout apology with a delighted giggle. "Did you see Vern all dressed up like a forty-niner? He didn't want to see the show they're putting on at the church and school—"

"Not a show," Stacy corrected her with mock gravity. "We are about to see 'a nostalgic vignette of the past.' It says so here on the program."

"Blah-blah-blah. Anyway, Vern told me to go and see it while he talks to a friend of his."

They walked together toward the school. The camera was turned on the door and the steps leading to a small platform. A schoolteacher in a prim, high-necked, long-sleeved dress stood in the doorway, ringing a bell which brought a small horde of children all garbed as children were a hundred years ago.

Stacy murmured to Eve, "Just imagine all the work all the mothers did, making those white pinafores for the girls to wear for just the minute or two for this act—or vignette—"

"Such gawky dresses they used to wear," Eve commented. "And how did the boys ever get around in those pants buttoned so tight at the knee?"

And now the bell began to ring in the church steeple. The camera focused on the church door and the knot of people exiting from the church. Shawled and bonneted women clasped prayer books. Men, dressed as cowhands or mule skinners, carried guns and bull whips. The group held their decorous pose only until the cameraman moved on.

Doc Bledsoe's wife was one of the churchgoers. She came over to Stacy to ask, "What happened to your sleeves?"

Stacy lingered to tell her the what and why of her missing sleeves and to hear the woman's fervent "I wish I could rip them out of this velvet basque. A mustard plaster couldn't be hotter."

Stacy was suddenly aware that the cameraman and Marcia Mills had moved on to the blacksmith shop. Eve must have gone too. Good heavens, and Stacy, still carrying the undelivered hoof trimmer.

She ran to the blacksmith shop and the crowd gathered there. The camera was already turning, and Marcia Mills, eyes bright with interest, kept up a running commentary into her mike. Some old gentleman looked down at Stacy to say in a high-pitched cackle, "This here is the real thing—I know—Yes, siree."

She pushed herself on through the enthusiastic crowd. The boys were doing themselves proud. There were the anvils she had been called on so often to admire. There was the forge full of red coals, and on them a horseshoe heating to a glowing pink. Even the paunchy white horse was tied to a corner of the building, and Enrico was cradling its hind foot in his aproned lap.

Stacy would still be able to slip him the hoof trimmer, because the camera at the moment was turned on Wild Bill and the red-hot horseshoe he was plucking off the coals with his tongs. She thrust the knife out to him. "Enrico, here's the trimmer from the Payne boy. It's sharp as a razor."

"Keep it. Don't give it to me now—not now," he jerked out without looking up. "My hands are shaking so—I could jab his Achilles tendon with it—Cripes—"

The cameraman motioned Stacy to stand aside so he could train his camera on the horseshoeing process. She moved away and waited. She knew, because the boys had told her, that the first part of their act was Enrico's trimming of the horse's hoof in readiness for the shoe. Then when Wild Bill put the red-hot shoe on the anvil, that was the cue for Enrico to take up his hammer and his position at the other anvil. And when both hammers were swinging in rhythm, the jolly blacksmiths were to break into the "Anvil Chorus."

Enrico put down the horse's hoof. He picked up his hammer and swung it. There now! Stacy, listening, could tell when the beat was right. She saw Wild Bill glance at Enrico, waiting for him to lead off so that he could add his weaker voice to the sound. Enrico opened his mouth—but no sound came. He swallowed hard, and opened his mouth again. Again, not a sound—

Suddenly into the air burst a loud rendering of "Pour me a tankard—"

Stacy stared in amazement at the shy, gangling, and right now, glassy-eyed Wild Bill who was responsible for that masterful bellow. A voice beside her said, "Godamighty, girlie, I didn't know he had it in him." Neither did Stacy. And to judge from the shocked look on his face, neither did Wild Bill himself.

But the hammers swung and rang, driving out the camera's hum. Marcia Mills, eyes alert, kept up her bright commentary into the mike.

Even after the two television workers moved on and the hammers were stilled, a large part of the crowd lingered. The men were especially interested in the equipment the boys had gathered together.

"When are you going to put a shoe on your horse?" Mr. McKibben asked Enrico.

"I got to get over the shakes first," he said.

Eve suddenly reappeared. "Vern doesn't want to see the Enos Starbrush museum, either. I saw Fabe, and he says just as soon as the TV folks finish with Enos's museum, it's going to close until the governor's speech is over, and he has to speechify right away so's he can get back to Denver and govern. Then they'll open the museum again, but let's go now and get it over with. Because Aunt Evvy would never forgive us if we didn't go through it and Oh and Ah over everything in it."

Stacy looked questioningly at Mr. McKibben. He had a certain pleased-with-himself cockiness since driving the stagecoach so creditably with the governor in the seat beside him. "All right, all right, guess we might as well go," he said. "Might as well see what all the women accomplished by running their legs off all summer."

Mrs. Payne was standing on the narrow front porch of the yellow Starbrush house. She was telling a group of tourists that the museum was closed now because of the governor's speech. She waited until they were out of hearing before telling Mr. McKibben and the two girls that, even though the front door was locked, they could go around and in the back. "Evvy's still there. But I'm going to hear what the governor has to say."

The three walked past the long wooden bench in back of the house that was now a museum. Two battered galvanized tubs, one with a washboard in it, sat on the bench. Eve shoved open the back door and they stepped into the narrow hall. The door on the left opened into the kitchen, the one on the right to the bedroom. The doorway straight ahead, and without a door on it, opened into the Starbrush parlor.

Stacy gave only a swift glance into the bedroom with its four-poster bed, patchwork quilt, and those twin pillow shams. (She had to admit they looked authentic and attractive.) She gave an even swifter glance in the kitchen at the shiny black stove with an iron teakettle on it and a rope clothesline strung over it, from which hung a man's long, red underwear, a woman's ruffled muslin drawers, and a baby dress with a crocheted yoke.

Mrs. McKibben was in the parlor. Stacy noticed again how lumpy and ungraceful Milly's mauve magenta hung. Or was it because its wearer was slumped by Milly's organ in utter dejection? Her arms were crossed over her middle as though she were shielding an ache.

Eve asked, "Well, did the TV people do a special feature on you seated at Milly's organ in Milly's dress like you planned?"

Numbly her aunt turned an empty, and somehow bruised face to the three. "No, they didn't. The girl didn't think it was worth bringing their heavy sound and film equipment inside." Her voice was very precise, but it too sounded empty and bruised. Stacy began to hurt for her.

The precise voice went on. "I heard her tell the cameraman that these old restored homes of a town's founders were a dime a dozen. She said their descendants always thought all the world was panting to see where they'd lived, but that her TV show had had more than enough of nutmeg graters and slop jars with pansies painted on them."

"That was mean—stinkin' mean—of her," Stacy broke out indignantly.

"Who does that frippery woman think she is anyway?" Mr. McKibben demanded. It was the closest Stacy had ever seen him direct his words *to* his wife. He repeated more angrily, "Yeh, just *who* does she think she is?"

She knows who she is. A gal with goals and ambitions of her own, Fabian had said.

Mrs. McKibben's flat and bruised voice went on, "I keep thinking of what she said. I guess maybe I did attach more importance to what was in the past." She wasn't looking at her husband, but Stacy knew that every word was *for* him. Maybe she was taking this way of admitting to herself and to him that neither did she know what she was trying to prove. "I thought it was more important than anyone else did. I mean, young Kenneth didn't think it was important enough to bring his wife down—"

"She's got hay fever," Eve put in.

"Her hay fever isn't that bad. I thought it would mean a lot to your father, Eve—He's my young—my only brother—" Her voice and lips were going a little wobbly. "But he just—joked about it. And now—now, it's over—and—" She tried to pull her features together but it was too late. She broke down. She held on to the carved music rack on Milly's old organ while sobs shook her.

Eve and Stacy moved swiftly to the kitchen. They were both sniffling and crying. But they stopped at the sound of a man's rumbling voice. They stood very still, and listened shamelessly. "Now, Evvy, now—don't cry—" She couldn't see the two in the Enos Starbrush parlor, but Stacy had a feeling that Mr. McKibben's hand was clumsily patting a shoulder covered by mauve-magenta poplin.

Very stealthily she and Eve slipped out the back door. Eve was the kind who could dry her tears quickly, and she did so now with a final sniff. "Well, it's about time those two stopped acting like adolescents are supposed to act."

"I wish Wild Bill had dropped that red-hot horseshoe on Marcia Mills's foot," Stacy said in a choked voice.

Eve said, "Vern's waiting for me," and went flying off in her bright red calico.

Stacy leaned a minute or two longer against the washbench with its round tubs, wiping her eyes and blowing her nose. And then she too went hurrying toward the crowd gathering about the bandstand to hear the governor's speech. She had to find Fabian.

She found him in the milling throng at the foot of the two steps leading to the platform. He was escorting a very old lady in a coffee-colored dress that smelled of camphor to a place of honor on the platform. She was the oldest citizen in the Starbrush country and one of the few who had known the founder. She included Stacy in the story she was telling Fabian, "—and that nice Mr. Starbrush picked me up and carried me across the muddy street—"

Because Stacy couldn't wholly trust the old lady's deafness, and because people were crowded close, she cupped her hand to Fabian's ear and whispered, "You'll never believe it!—the ice jam is broken."

He backed away a step and looked at her with unbelieving eyes. "I can't believe it. Are you sure?"

"Sure as God made little green apples."

The pleased old lady kept on with her story, "—yes, as nice as you please, he carried me in his arms across the street—my, oh, my, the mud—and he put me down—"

The governor himself, all vote-getting folksiness, leaned down to take the oldest citizen's other arm and assist Fabian in getting her up the steps. He had only time to wink at Stacy.

But Centennial Day was half over. Tomorrow and the trip to Denver and the stopover at Pigeon Rock were that much closer.

20

The next morning Stacy slowed the station wagon to cross the railroad tracks into Starbrush. The town, which had been so crowded and noisy and colorful yesterday, was just now yawning and stretching itself awake. A desultory breeze whipped some of the pink programs through the streets—like strewn and mussed flower petals.

"Go straight on through—straight through," Mr. McKibben said. "You don't need to stop for anything, Fabian?"

"Not now. Not with the Centennial over and done with." There was an amen in his voice.

"How about you, girlie? You want to say good-bye to your quiz kids?"

She shook her head. Yesterday had been a time of good-byes.

The climax of yesterday's Centennial celebration had been the barbecued buffalo supper served on the grounds of Enos Park by the volunteer firemen. But a sudden wind that swirled paper plates and napkins, with a spate of rain that dampened tables and their attached benches, food and the partakers of it, had hastened departures.

Judge McKibben, possessed of that same restlessness as his father, had eaten hurriedly, said his good-byes, given Stacy a check for her summer's work along with appreciative words, and departed. Eve's father had left soon afterward.

Marcia Mills hadn't bothered with good-byes to anyone. Not even to Fabian, he admitted when Stacy questioned him. The camera and mike had been turned on the governor only long enough for his opening tribute to the fearless pioneers *and* one Enos Starbrush. Then she, her cameraman, equipment, and station wagon were gone. Stacy wondered if she might be covering another of her dime-a-dozen Centennial Days.

Stacy ate supper with the blacksmiths. She was able to brave the brief shower by their contributing one leather apron for her to sit on and the other to pull over her shoulders. The hoof trimmer was used to carve a watermelon into wedges, and they tried to see who could spit seeds the farthest.

They told her the sobering news that Wild Bill was to go up before the draft board the following week, and Enrico on the tenth of September. They gave her a horseshoe for good luck—the very one that had glowed red on the forge while the movie camera clicked. They both kissed her good-bye, and promised to love her forever and ever.

And all the time her heart was registering

every move Fabian made. He wasn't eating. He was hustling about, looking troubled and apologetic as though he were responsible for the wind blowing hats off heads and balloons out of children's hands.

There had been more good-byes this morning. All Stacy's squabbles with Eve were forgotten. They held each other close and wiped away tears. "Come and see us in Denver, Eve, and stay for a week."

"I will—you bet I will. I'd go right in with you and Fabe and Uncle Mac this morning, only Vern's coming out tonight and bringing his records." She added low, "Besides Aunt Ev hasn't paid me yet."

"Good-bye, Mrs. McKibben."

"Good-bye, Stacy." Just a certain amount of thawing, but no miraculous warming. Not even a peck on the cheek, but a brief handshake and a flick of smile. "I'm sorry I never got around to making another one of those chocolate tortes you liked so well."

Nor had there been any miraculous warmth displayed between the two heads of the house. At breakfast Mrs. McKibben poured coffee at her end of the table; Mr. McKibben, at his, gave Vrest instructions for the two or three days he would be gone. In fact, they were both careful *not* to speak to each other.

So that in the brief moment when Fabian took Stacy's bulging Mexican bag from her, she whispered, "Honest, Fabian, they did speak yesterday there by the organ in the Enos Starbrush parlor. Just like I told you. Why don't they now?"

"Because they'd feel a little foolish in front of all of us, I suppose."

"He went back after his checkbook. Maybe he's kissing her good-bye."

"Stacy the incurable romantic."

Fabian also had a present for Stacy. A yucca plant in a flowerpot. "Ugly-looking thing now, but you plant it in your yard, and next year you'll have a bloom of waxen, tulip-shaped candleholders on it."

"You said they were like chalices."

"Yes, chalices for sun and rain—and hope. You were holding one that morning you jumped on me—remember?—and accused me of plotting to get rid of you."

Again that near stitch in her side made her catch her breath. *And you said you didn't want me to get hurt. Oh, hurry, Mr. McKibben, so we can get started. So we can get to Pigeon Rock.*

Stacy drove past Ethel's Eat Shop with the orange sign, "Bus Stop." On past the feed store, and Lindstrom's garage. The sound of bawling cattle came from the stockyards. Had it been only ten weeks since the day she had first driven down Starbrush's Main Street? It seemed as though a great chunk of her life had been spent here.

They reached Pigeon Rock at noon. Again Stacy parked in a splotch of shade along courthouse square. And again—oh, praise be!—Mr.

McKibben, with a mutter about seeing Dan Sweeney, left them. Stacy and Fabian went into the café.

The boy, who had waited on them before, recognized Stacy and asked her if she wanted tea. Fabian suggested, "Why don't you have a cold drink here, Stacy, and then real tea out of that big earthen pot when you get home?"

"Somebody broke the lid of it a long time ago," she remembered, "and we have to put a sauce-dish on for a top, and remember to hold it on. The littles always forget."

Fabian ordered sandwiches for both and coffee for himself. He bought a Denver paper and sat studying the want ads under "Trailers and Campers for Sale." He'd feel for the handle of his cup without taking his eyes off the page.

She tried to draw him into conversation by asking about his ducks. He answered absently that Arnold would take food to them until his grandmother got back next week. "She planned to be there for the Centennial, but she had car trouble." He went on reading.

She tried again. "Don't you think it was mean of Marcia Mills not to even take a picture of Mrs. McKibben in the Starbrush parlor?"

"Not mean. Just typical Marcia," he said, and turned a page.

Time was passing. Stacy said, "It's pretty stuffy in here. It'll be cooler in the car."

She got in behind the wheel, and Fabian sat

behind her, leaving Mr. McKibben his place in the front seat. Fabian encircled an ad on his folded paper with his ball-point. I'll look at this one first," he said, and read it to her. "1956 Chevy trailer toter complete."

She had to get his mind off whatever a trailer toter was. She said, "Fabian, I want to tell you something."

He looked at her with the disguised impatience he must often have shown when a student interrupted his thinking. She faltered out, "You mean—so much—to me. I'll always remember your giving me that slimsy little book and saying—"

"*Slimsy*! That's perfect, because it was slim and a little flimsy. I'd like to do a piece someday on how apt and fitting coined words can be."

"—and it was the most gladsome summer of my whole life."

"It's been gladsome for me too. You've no idea how happy it made me to get you started reading—and without my usual yammer to students about books opening doors, about books being the legacy of all mankind—"

"That first day when we sat here, you said you wouldn't insult a girl by asking her to marry you. You said you had, and the girl laughed at you. But that was Marcia, and I'm not like her. If I loved somebody, I wouldn't care if he was poor, or if I had to wait, or if I had to go to work to help. I would even quit school and go to work—"

"I'm sure you would, young'un."

"Don't call me young'un," she flared. "It makes me sound so idiot young—and foolish. What difference does age make? My father was what the O'Byrnes called *booky*—like you—and he was six years older than Mom, and they were so happy together. And I've grown up years and years this summer."

His eyes behind his glasses rested on her, puzzled and intent. And then, as though he found the answer in her flushed face and the incoherent words he had listened to, he looked away from her, up the street. He said, "There's Mr. McKibben now, coming out of the Red Horse."

Oh,, no! Why couldn't he have put his feet up and relaxed with Dan Sweeney with no thought of time as he had before? She watched him turn back to talk further with his friend in the doorway.

It was a reprieve but a brief one. Stacy said on a hurried breath, "That day it hailed, and we ate duck eggs and the rainbow was like our rainbow from heaven—"

"Wait, Stacy, wait. I want to ask you something. That first day when Judge McKibben came out to see you, and you saw me in the back seat of the car, what did you think of me?"

The unexpectedness of his question nonplussed her. She didn't answer. She couldn't very well tell him the truth.

He chuckled knowingly. "You're too nice to

tell me. You thought, 'Look at that mousy, booky fellow. He's not my dish.' "

She corrected him on a ragged laugh, "No, I thought owlish and schoolteacherish."

"And you were right. I *am* owlish and schoolteacherish, along with being mousy."

"How did you know I thought that?"

"From the expression on your face. You gave me one look, but not a second."

"So did you," she defended. "You looked up from your book and then went back to whatever it was."

"It was *Petals That Fall*, and I couldn't help comparing—"

She broke in. "What did you think of me?"

"I thought, There's a girl that'll get a lot out of life. Blessings and bruises. She'll get knocked down, but she'll bounce back. I couldn't help comparing you to Milly and her laments—mewlings, as Mr. Mac calls them—and her wallowing in all her unrequited love, instead of—"

"What does unrequited mean?"

"Unrequited love means love that isn't returned. Of course, Longfellow tells us in *Evangeline* that love given out—returned or not—is never wasted. That it returns to enrich the giver."

Mr. McKibben had taken a step or two down the street, but was detained again by some remark of Sweeney's.

Stacy said in a woebegone voice, "I don't want to leave you, Fabian."

He reached over from his back seat and patted her shoulder. "Life is full of leaving," he said gently. "And yet when two people mean something to each other, each one leaves something of himself with the other. You'll be a different person because you knew me this summer, and I'll be different for knowing you."

"How will you be different?" she asked, biting her twisting lips.

He thought aloud. "I'll be closer to life and people, because you showed me what it was like to care a lot. I'll remember you and your gladsome times and—" He chuckled. "—your madsome ones too. Yes, I'm apt to be a sidelines person. Maybe it's pure selfishness; maybe it's because I'm afraid of being hurt—" He talked on about books being good but not as a substitute for living.

Words, words, words. He was talking to keep her from saying more. He was pretending that he didn't know she had thrown herself at him. In his kind way he had given her to understand that he didn't love her or need her. And even that he doubted that what she felt for him was love. He had mentioned that afternoon of the hailstorm that fatherless girls were apt to have crushes on men teachers.

She sat drenched in misery and watched Mr. McKibben's jaunty and jerky gait as he crossed the quiet street and came toward them. He opened the car door. "Let's get on—let's get on now. Danny and I were talking, and he says he doesn't see why I can't make a beeline for the police station. He says there's no reason why I couldn't jostle that bunch of public servants down there into giving me my license back today. Let's go, girlie—let's go."

21

She was home again. Fabian had lost no time in depositing her Mexican bag at the front door because Mr. McKibben, after squeezing her hand and promising to keep in touch with her, was again tapping his booted foot and saying, "Let's get on now—let's get on downtown, Fabian."

A good-bye handshake from Fabian.

No one came rushing to open the front screen and hold it open for her. Not even Cully was there to overwhelm her with his greeting. Stacy stood on their front porch and glanced around. Goodness, how small and hemmed-in the patch of lawn around their house looked. How squeezed close together the houses on Hubbell Street looked. And how skimpy that elm in their yard was, compared to the wide-spreading, thick-trunked cottonwood in front of the McKibben house on the plains.

She picked up her striped bag and maneuvered it, herself, flowerpot, and horseshoe through the front door. Goodness, how shabby and cramped the rooms were. And how battered their old upright in the hall. She called out, but no one answered. She was glad for the empty house. She wanted to be alone and cry out her heartbreak.

She started up the stairs with her load. But she stopped on the landing, suddenly too weighted and weary to do anything but drop down. . . . She had dreamed of coming in that very front door, hand in hand with Fabian, and announcing, "We're in love, and I don't care how long I have to wait—" . . .

Fabian didn't want her to wait. And it was not "We're in love," but "I'm in love." What was the word he had used? *Unrequited,* which meant unreturned. She remembered the words from some opera, "End the pangs, the pangs of unrequited love." But her pangs would never end. They would always be there, like dry stones under her ribs. She cried in hurt and desolation.

Slumped there on the landing, she seemed to see the ghost of that slaphappy Stacy who ten weeks ago had come leaping joyously down these same stairs with the bag flapping against her knees. The weary and weighted Stacy turned tear-blotted eyes on her. *"It's all right for you to have all that bounce to the ounce. But then you've never lived with someone that didn't like you or want you. You've never been scared of wind and blackness because you didn't count any more than a fence post. No, and you've never read a book, and been so carried away by it that you forgot where you were."*

The prancy Stacy answered back, "Then what are you sitting there sniffling and moaning about?"

"You wouldn't understand. You don't even know that hearts can shatter. But they can. Mine is."

"Oh, that's awful. But a heart doesn't have to stay shattered for always and always,, does it?"

A shadow darkened the rectangle of screen door. Stacy sat up and wiped her eyes on the tail of her wraparound skirt. She heard that certain thud that she recognized as a fist thumping itself into a baseball mitt. The door opened and, before she could identify which of the littles came in, a whirlwind of dog was thumping his tail against her bare legs, licking her chin, and knocking over the flowerpot and contents. She fought herself free of him and said, "Hello, Brian. Where's everybody?"

"We kids are playing baseball. Only they made me bring Cully home because you know how when we run for a base, he runs too and gets in everybody's way."

"Where's Mom?"

"She didn't think you'd be home so soon. She went up to Pearl's bakery to get some of these little teeny-like pies—"

"Tarts."

"Yeh, for tea. Strawberry ones, because you like them. She had Pearl make her some because you were coming home."

"Brian, do I look older and—different?"

"Not very much. Your nose is peeling, and Jill used up all the nose-peeling salve. What are you going to do with all your money?"

"I don't know. I haven't thought about it." *I've been so busy thinking about Fabian, and right now all he can think about is a trailer toter.*

The old bubbly Stacy nudged her. *Remember?—you're going to buy everybody everything his or her heart desires.*

Brian started for the door, then turned back to say, "Did you read what I wrote on the idiot board for you?"

She shook her head. The idiot board hung right outside the kitchen and over the telephone where messages were scribbled. She supposed the family thought she would run and scan it eagerly the minute she came in. The old boy-crazy Stacy would have.

"I wrote down what this fellow that plays the guitar told me to when he phoned."

"Pete's his name." But that was aeons ago that she had danced with a boy with an untidy thatch of dark hair and listened to his talk about his Sing Outers—and didn't he say he wrote songs too? She righted the flowerpot Cully had knocked over, and listlessly brushed up the spilled dirt into her palm and shook it back in.

"That funny-looking thing in the pot isn't marijuana, is it?"

"Shame on you, Brian. It's a yucca—soapweed, they call them out there—and it looks like it's dead, but in the spring it has a whole bunch of white flowers and—and a fellow I know said they were ivory chalices to catch the—the sun—"

There went the pangs of unrequited love. Pangs *hurt*. Like a sore throat, only all the way down to her middle.

"Where'd you get the horseshoe? What you going to do with it?"

"I don't know." *And I don't care.*

"They're lucky, aren't they?"

This time the old Stacy who believed in luck answered for her, "Yes, and this one is specially lucky, so we'll hang it on the front door and then the whole house will be lucky."

Brian said, "I guess I better get back to where we're playing baseball, because this isn't my glove. It's Dub's, and he'll be having a conniption if—"

"Don't you have a baseball mitt of your own?"

Out of his superior wisdom, he corrected her gently, "This isn't a mitt. It's a fielder's finger glove." He added reverently, "It's a Ted Williams' personal model. None of us littles could have one like this. Dub has got a real rich uncle that bought it for his birthday."

The exuberant Stacy was saying, but not aloud because it would be fun to surprise him, *Hah, me lad, I guess you've forgotten that you've got a real rich sister.*"

And suddenly the old, but green and untouched, Stacy was no longer on the landing. Nor was the weary heavy-hearted returnee. The two had merged into one being. Was that what living was, what growing up was? Was it changing into a different person as you went through life, yet still keeping the old core, the old identity, the old *you*?

Brian was carefully edging himself through a small opening of screen door. "Don't let Cully get out, will you?"

She got up and latched the screen after him so Cully couldn't shove it open. She hurried to close the back door too. All the familiar things of home began moving back into their old perspective. It didn't seem as though she had been gone for ten weeks. It seemed as though she had only left a day or so ago. She was scolding Cully as she always did. "Just stop your whining—because you're not getting out." And looking in the bread box and saying, "Here's a Fig Newton for you."

She turned her attention to the idiot board. Brian had written:

"He said to sweepe off fron steps so he can sit ther and play he's gutter."

She had no laugh in her yet, but she half smiled at that "gutter." She felt hollow and dry of throat. She would make the tea and surprise Mother when she came home with the tarts. Ben would be driving in soon too.

She put on the teakettle, and reached for the big earthenware teapot. She stood holding it and breathed out, "I'll buy Mom a new one, so we won't have to use a saucedish in the top, and we won't have to hold it in when it's so hot it burns your finger, and so the littles won't forget and let another saucedish drop out and break. Yes, siree." This time her pleased smile was a whole one.

She would have time for a quick shower while the water came to a boil. She glanced inside the downstairs bath under the stairs, and saw a new kind of shampoo. She'd wash her dusty hair too. *He had said her wet hair was the color of a copper kettle.* She waited for the pain to come. It came, but not quite as sharp or as lasting as before.

She stepped out of her clothes and turned the shower on full blast. Who could take a shower without singing in it? She had no idea of what she tra-la-laed, or whether it had words or not. It was the music the rock band had played at the Auf Wiedersehen prom when she had danced with a brown-eyed boy with devil-may-care eyes. And the words had to do with not giving all your love away, but saving some for a rainy day—tra-la-la—de-da—da-de-da—

About the Author

Lenora Mattingly Weber was born in Dawn, Missouri. When she was twelve, her adventurous family set out to homestead on the plains of Colorado. There she raised motherless lambs on baby bottles, gentled broncos, and chopped railroad ties into firewood. At the age of sixteen she rode in rodeos and Wild West shows. Her well-loved stories for girls reflect her experiences with her own family. As the mother of six children and as a grandmother, she is well qualified to write of family life. Her love of the outdoors, her interest in community affairs, and her deep understanding of family relationships all help to make her characters as credible as they are memorable.

Mrs. Weber still enjoys horseback riding and swimming. She loves to cook, but her first love is writing.